SHAME

SHAME

GRANT MAIERHOFER

FC2
TUSCALOOSA

The University of Alabama Press
Tuscaloosa, Alabama 35487-0380

FC2 is an imprint of the University of Alabama Press

Inquiries about reproducing material from this work should be addressed to the University of Alabama Press

Book Design: Publications Unit, Department of English, Illinois State University; Director: Steve Halle, Production Assistant: Alex Wright
Cover Design: Lou Robinson
Typeface: Adobe Jenson Pro

Library of Congress Cataloging-in-Publication Data is available from the Library of Congress.

ISBN: 978-1-57366-194-2

E-ISBN: 978-1-57366-896-5

Contents

In the Time
When the Americans
Decided Certain Things
Were Thus   1

    In the Time
    When My Memory
    Fixated on the Death
    of Princess Diana   29

        In the Time
        of Paternity
        and the Volvo 240 Wagon   69

           In the Time
           of Death   93

               In the Time
               of Grant Maierhofer,
               Old and Sick   137

Fiction, of events and facts strictly real; autofiction, if you will, to have entrusted the language of an adventure to the adventure of language, outside of the wisdom and the syntax of the novel, traditional or new. Interactions, threads of words, alliterations, assonances, dissonances, writing before or after literature, concrete, as we say, music.

—Serge Doubrovsky, on the back cover of *Fils*

IN THE TIME
WHEN THE AMERICANS
DECIDED CERTAIN THINGS
WERE THUS

(I need your love)
(I need your love)
(I need your love)
(I need your love)
"Guilt is a Useless Emotion," New Order

1.

For a long time I was unmedicated and went to bed at the appropriate hour. I started medication when I was seven and my sleep has been erratic and strange ever since, mostly leaving me dead to the world for most of the time and sleeping as much as I can. I don't much remember the sleep of my youth except for the bed where I slept and the blankets I used. I remember a thing I used to do when we would go to Kwik Trip and we were allowed one drink and one piece of candy which we'd then eat in a dark basement watching a movie. I would buy a bag of grape Big League Chew bubble gum and I would get the largest fountain cup they had and fill it with a little bit of every kind of soda. I did this once since then and it tasted the exact same. A cup containing all sorts of colors and sugars and diet carcinogens that I'd drink slowly and savor and I could almost delude myself into thinking I could taste what was what as I drank the entire thing over the course of the film. I didn't get sick then or have rotgut. I didn't feel panicky from the caffeine. It was summer and it was hot outside and everything in the world started and ended with that nice cool basement where we'd talk about whatever we watched and make jokes and become entirely caught up in what happened on screen. It was a form of trance that I think I've been seeking since. There's no real way of looking at memory. It's a sea behind us, this ugly wave of mistake and regret. All of it ready at any moment to come right back and attain exact relevance without warning. It's there, always. Some days I cling to it more aggressively and it makes things move with a jagged stupidity. Others I'm in the moment and I'm panicking, always panicking. My days now are consumed with bits of work and my family and my children and not much else. I'll sit glued to screens as much as I can manage. I'll walk around a little or feed the dog. I like to get lost in the days and I miss the ability to travel.

2.

I'd started the meditations in the early morning when my family
was all asleep and just before we were staying at Mother's house in
Wisconsin. I'd read from some of the original Buddhist texts and
found something that surprised me, and since reading it I couldn't
stop wanting to pursue it. It was a passage about imagining one's
death. Not just the absence of yourself on earth, but the actual moment when you're pushed from the living to the dead, and you're
meant to linger on that for as long as you can. The passage re-
fers to being shot full of arrows, or choking on one's own vomit,
or being strangled to death, or starving, or being trapped beneath
thick layers of ice in frigid waters, or being burned in a roaring
fire. I skimmed these texts basically, looking occasionally for things
that stood out that might help me. I'd found this one the day after
we got the call that Father had passed, and had tried ruminating
on my own death at length on the plane ride home, and had kept
doing so, often while I took a shower and we prepared to face another day filled with relatives in mourning and in grief. I didn't
know what would come from it, and I don't think I cared. For the
first time that I could remember, I was inside my life, within the
moment. I don't know how else to say that. I don't think it matters
much. I just remember the various shrieks that would come from

various mouths and the quiet and dark of the plane and my life laid out there in front of me in structures, and I could watch it there, at rest.

3.

Before the first meditation on the trip we were sitting at the airport in Seattle with our children who were dozing off in car seats or sitting flipping through books they'd brought for the trip. I was flipping through the books I had on my phone and settled on a large PDF I'd downloaded of original writings by various monks. I'd found the passage and was poring over it as we boarded the plane and got our children settled for the flight back to Minneapolis. When I was younger the thought of death was semantic. Things die. We die. People die constantly, every single day. When I began assembling this document, then, and when I started to look at my life and see things a bit more clearly, the death meditations seemed capable of transporting me back to that earlier version of myself, real or fictive, regardless of perspective or voice, and I could feel at peace there like I had when I was younger, sitting in the middle of a classroom surrounded by people I couldn't understand but wanted to so desperately. They would come to my house and spend time with me and I would want so desperately to embody them. I was assembling the document in their honor. I am not interested in a new way of looking at the world, or at life. I do not hope to find an openness in the work. I only hope for my small life to mete itself out in minor steps in no particular direction as the noise of it gets ever quieter and quieter. Before I'm old and shitting my-self and watching the same film over and over and over while my family awkwardly whispers in the kitchen, I'll throw myself from some window. I'll find it, any building anywhere, and go as far up as I'm able, and I'll make myself a minor news story in the evening. Defenestration and the noise of my life will be forever quieted, the matter of my flesh buried without a box underground with two acorns scattered over it and my legacy to be forgotten. I don't hold onto this world. I don't hold onto life. You don't hold onto some-thing that wrongs you and continues to do so. You let it sleep like the noise of your mind and living and you wander out some day and set it free as you turn back to the middling existence you've established there.

4.

In the first meditation I was sitting alone on a night flight as my daughters and son sat across the aisle with my wife and they were sound asleep. I closed my eyes and began to imagine the plane having difficulty. This quickly progressed to the plane being on fire and everyone panicking around me. I sat there in my mind looking around at chaos as the plane was a blur of fire and lights and the captain shrieked to us over the loudspeaker that we were going down somewhere over Montana, that they would try and land us in a body of water soon enough to get us safely on the ground. Sometimes the only way through to calm on flights for me was to engage catastrophe very directly, even before the meditation—and probably not just on flights. The news that Father was dead came in the morning. I had been partially sleeping as I take a large dose of antipsychotic medication each night to ease my obsessive-compulsive disorder. In the mornings sometimes I'm a nuisance for my wife to wake up. That morning I was asleep and then my phone rang and it was Mother, and she was crying. Father had called me the day before in the afternoon.

5.

I called my first book *Ode to a Vincent Gallo Nightingale* because the publisher thought that title was good. The book was this thin collection of poems and I'd been obsessed with Vincent Gallo. I remember my sister calling me while I waited to go into a movie and she told me she'd watched *Buffalo '66* with her boyfriend and he'd said he wanted to understand more of Christina Ricci's character. It seemed to me to be a film about Gallo's character. I called the book that because I identified with that character. I don't think I was ready to marry my wife until our daughter was born and I don't think I was ready to grow in any manner until we'd gotten married. I think it's a bad title. The more children you have the bigger the effect is on you as a human being. Being married changes you. These things are obvious to most people I think. I think the wrong things are obvious to me. I don't know why I called my first book that. I'm not sure whether I wrote it. I'm not sure which parts of it I wrote.

6.

Father was on a boat in Greece, traveling from one island to another where he was going to spend the day, sitting in the sun painting pictures of the local foliage and a bunch of cats that snuck around the island between its occupants' legs, we spoke while he was on the boat, I couldn't hardly hear him. Around twelve hours later, I think, Mother got word that he had died in the night, and so Mother called my wife and me in the morning, and she was crying. I don't exactly know why, but I didn't cry. I wanted to cry. I didn't feel as though I was in shock. I didn't know what being in shock would feel like. I just felt odd about everything then. Someone my sister worked with was going to pay for our flights home. I contacted my boss at the university where I was working. They said don't worry. Take all the time you need. This is more important. Email your students when you can and come back when things are in order. I remember feeling as though I was getting away with something. We hung around for a day and then we flew back to Minneapolis to commune and figure things out as they concerned Father's passing. I believe these are moments where being coached would be easier, having someone tell you what to do. I wanted to cry. I didn't though. It's unsettling, looking at yourself and knowing you're not doing the proper thing. It's a common sensation for me but on days when things are more pronounced it's completely destabilizing. I needed to cry.

7.

Literature is a game of Telephone. You sit down and you do your best to describe the absolute hell of living within your mind. You hand it to the person next to you who is dealing with the impossible hell of living within their mind. They take what they can from it, and look within, and they turn around and pass it to someone else, who will in turn apply its relevance to the hell of living within their mind, and the two of them might turn back and talk to the author in a language the author can't understand, about the impossible hell of living within their minds. It's not that art is just subjective. Living is just subjective. People like to talk about art as this thing that affords empathy, a chance to engage someone's experience and broaden their purview. My experience has been the opposite of this. The more I read the more likely I am to live that much more aggressively and contentedly within the impossible hell of living in my mind. I think that this is a good thing. I think that writers who talk about writing and empathy are delusional. I think that anyone who talks about art and empathy is delusional. The problem is that our subjectivity makes us all delusional, and my own take on anything is as meaningless and useless as the language someone might use to try and engage with me about the impossible hell of living within their mind. I think that I am delusional.

8.

I don't know if this fed into my feelings when I was told Father died. I know we stayed where we lived in Idaho for a day until our flight was ready but I have no idea what we did that day. I think we probably looked at our phones. I remember taking a shower and crying a little but it felt forced. I don't remember what my wife and I talked about. I think we talked about how strange it was. I think we talked about how I had just spoken with him. I realized then that I processed things wrong. I think I knew this about myself to a degree, but this put it plainly in front of me. As a drug addict, an alcoholic, a depressive, an obsessive, and a chronically anxious person, I processed things wrong. Good and bad made me want to drink and use, mild made me want to drink and use. Good and bad made me certain I was useless and despicable, mild made me certain I was useless and despicable. It all did. I couldn't read the world. I hadn't kept anyone close because I didn't want to look at these things directly. I wanted to just keep going until I died in some minor, stupid way. I don't know when I have and when I haven't been a dry drunk, or whether it matters. I remember apologizing a lot, then apologizing a lot more. My wife is someone I learned to keep close, but there were also lots of errors on my part in that pursuit. I fail in most moments of my life.

9.

I remember being in rehab and there was this guy named Al there and some sort of event was going on one day and Al and I realized they were serving full-caffeine coffee—it was rehab, and they'd let us smoke, minors or not, but they didn't need everybody standing around the coffee dispenser like fiends—and so Al and I were refilling these complimentary mugs they gave us all day and we kept passing one another and smiling knowingly. If I could still communicate with anybody from rehab or the halfway house he'd be the one. I think that night we all drove in big vans to Center City where the Hazelden for adults (the original Hazelden) was, and we had this big dinner and watched a speaker in this nice auditorium. We ate pretty well at the Hazelden in Plymouth, but this was more of a feast. Some of the moments in rehab were the best in my life. I was there in March and into the summer. Yearning for that state has kept me sober. Being happier kept me sober in rehab. Two of my roommates cheeked their meds one night and snorted them. I could've joined them, but I stayed clean because I'd found a happiness in staying clean that I'd never felt before. It's fleeting but even a glimpse of it now will warm me over for days. After rehab in the halfway house in Wayzata, Minnesota I worked at a grocery store down the street. I would walk to work every day smoking and then I'd work and I'd do my job and hide in the bathroom and when I got breaks I'd eat and smoke and drink coffee. One day after work I'd gotten paid and I bought a rotisserie chicken and a jug of mango juice and I walked down the street eating it and I felt free.

10.

Nothing prepares you for having children. Raising children is impossible. Every single day you're shown some ugly depth in yourself of frustration or fear, or something less concrete. Every single day the beauty of your children brings with it an absolute horror of losing them, in any capacity. Nobody tells you that your worst qualities will be amplified tenfold. When I was alone I would get angry. I would walk around picking fights with the air and there could be no end to it and that would be fine. Now my anger is pathetic. I don't know if life gets better. I am afraid. I am constantly afraid. I'm on more medicine now than I've ever been on in my entire life and in rehab they handed out medicine generously. All they talk about when they talk about any of this is useless. They tell you to work hard. They tell you to make time for you. They tell you if the house hasn't burned down you're doing alright. Nothing prepares you for it, and nothing makes things simpler. They tell you everything they can in their last effort of righting their own lives.

11.

I hope that Father was somewhere beautiful the day before he died. I hope he had a nice large meal, laughed with the workers and people he'd met. I hope he was able to drink and eat. I hope that he was happy in his hotel room as the night took shape. And I hope that he was resting softly in a large bed in Greece, the windows open just a bit and the air from the city coming in, as he passed into the night. My sense of all of it is wrong. My sense of all this is wrong. A person goes to sleep, and doesn't wake up, and is gone from life, and we're back here, trying to figure anything of it out. The plague overwhelming things. In the year 1666 Pepys is frantically scribbling, London is on fire, the great plague is overwhelming everything, and Newton is watching an apple fall near to where some bodies are buried and the world is collapsing as they know it. There's no further reading to do.

12.

I don't know about guilt, or shame. I want guilt to be a useless emotion. When I was alone I spent as much time as I could asleep, or watching something, or reading, or masturbating, or doing other things to quiet my mind. Now I'm on medication and I'll have this tendency to dwell and then I'll talk to my doctor and they'll alter a dose. I don't know if it has been as clear as that. I don't know if I'm on too much medication. I don't want that to be the case. I don't want to be abusing things. I don't think I am. It's never very far off. There's always that potential in me. I know that nothing is truly free from the addict. I can, and do, become addicted to things that aren't even tangible. A thought, a little sense of myself, an image there of what I might've been—unlived lives, made-up histories, conversations I haven't had, acts of violence I haven't experienced—all the little fragments linger there awaiting the addict in my head. The addict is my head. A little saucer of milk to dip my open eyeballs in could be the thing. Walking backwards could be the thing. Reading user's manuals could be the thing. It doesn't matter. It hasn't mattered. Anything could be the thing and that's this reality. It doesn't matter.

13.

I breathed in and out slowly, filling my chest and diaphragm as deeply with air as I could. I thought about those I've known who've died. A friend. His name was Ed. He was kind and strange. I spent days with him when I was a teenager. We spent all day drinking and walking around Eau Claire. I hugged him. We went to a show and he wrapped his arm around me. I can be such a coward. I long to be in that day with Ed. We'd gotten a case of beer. We went to this friend's apartment who wasn't home. Ed drank and kicked a half-full can of beer up at a clock on the wall. We listened to music. We drank, did drugs, we smoked. We went out after that and into the early afternoon sun, walking around dressed in our boots and our leathers and our ripped jeans. We talked about all kinds of things, anxious but living more through it. There was a show that night, we'd be next to our friends and we'd drink some more or take some drugs and there was a purity in that. Later, I walked around Wayzata, Minnesota with my roommate the second day in my halfway house. We smoked, and talked, and got food, and got coffee, and told fucked-up jokes, and applied for jobs, and it was deeply human, and the two in their way are the same. That night I think a group of us watched a film. My roommate and I had walked down the street to Blockbuster and rented it. We went to a meeting later, and that communion sustained us. These are the moments I think I've come to search for, through the presence of other miserable people.

14.

I remember finding out about the death of someone once. I'd known them when I was younger. They'd taken their own life. The narrative reached us in a scattered way so that we were following two deaths simultaneously all day, until at the end of the day we realized both deaths were the same—and it was someone we'd known—and they'd taken their own life in this very horrific way in response to a situation that was unfathomably extreme, to us. I had spent the summer day with my friends and then they left after we had pieced much of it together, but it wasn't until I heard my sister collapse upstairs into unrestrained weeping that everything got clear, and I felt entirely removed from whatever sense I'd previously had of the stability of being. That someone who was always right there could possess these things, this death, it seemed alien. Another death was similar, a girl I'd known had moved someplace else, and had ended her life with her partner, and the somberness of the event wouldn't leave me for days. Anything you hold onto vanishes with death, perhaps especially with suicide. Mostly leaving this world seems sensible, but that sensibility holds an entry point to stuff beyond that suicide, which makes the suicide all the more horrid to comprehend. We know they were capable of accessing that impossibility, but the repeated beatings of living was equally strong, and so they leave, and who could argue with it. Life is re-lentless in its torture of all forms of matter, and so finding death the last viable gesture when living has so disappointed someone, is perhaps rational. Still, we want to hold them and stave off life.

15.

I remember the low din of voices and the occasional expression of pain or discomfort, met with more low hums of people attempting to ease the pain of whoever spoke. The town where I grew up was a bland place. A video exists of a reporter in front of my high school talking about Mary Brunner, one of the Manson family members, who had returned to the Midwest after everything was said and done and had started to raise a family, or something. That's about all I'd care for anybody to know about the place. Not out of any bitterness but out of the sense that that's about all anybody need know about any place. The fetishization of various places in the world has become this pathetic tendency people have to make their lived days more significant by tying them to some sense of New York, or LA, or whatever. People in the country feel as though they're missing something in the city because people seem to *know* certain things there, but nobody anywhere knows anything significant that anybody couldn't learn anywhere else. We're all just telling ourselves bad stories, trying to find significance in our lived experience and sending occasional distress signals that are answered with further distress signals which in turn offer not much of anything back. I guess I've grown tired of any sort of exceptionalism. I have simple, unmarked hands that haven't worked or been put to anything significant but that's fine. I'm not exceptional or very different from anyone else. We're the same miserable idiots.

16.

I remember the night I told Father that my first bad novel was going to be published. I went into his room there and told him that my first bad novel was going to be published. He hugged me and he said that he was proud of me. I don't remember exactly what he said but I think that's close. My first bad novel was published and it received one incredibly kind review that I don't understand. It seems to be about a different book. There are things I could admit about myself that would make me irredeemable. I think most days that we've all got these things, though I'm not certain. I've had moments in my life that I'm deeply ashamed of. I've tried to use that shame to cease behaviors I'm ashamed of. My anger has led to things I'd be deeply ashamed to share with most people. This was the beginning of the time when Americans had started to publicly shame people based on their indiscretions. In some cases it led to situations where people were able to air past grievances, and highlight the repeated bad behaviors of apparent sociopaths who showed no interest in changing their approach to being a person in the world. I found myself talking to my therapist about Christ, and thinking about things I'd done when I was younger, people I'd hurt, even as far back as when I was in elementary school, and I became obsessed with the notion of being shamed, and this occupied all my days, except when I would watch TV at night and my brain would stop moving. I had done things I deeply regretted, and I had behaved badly or cruelly, but I did not see myself as a uniquely evil being. I was trying. I was failing. I spent a lot of time thinking I would go to prison. Then, though, I thought about prison. People locked away for mistakes made when impulsive or thoughtless. They sober up in prison, maybe. They get therapy, sure. They read. If someone got out of prison after doing the vilest thing I could imagine, and then showed true contrition, and decided to devote their life to making things better for as many people as they could and to help victims, would I ignore this person? Would I disregard everything they had to say? Although their crime might be unforgivable, I would listen. I would even read a book they wrote, or watch a film they created, or look at a painting they made. Being in recovery makes you reacquaint yourself daily with what the gnarled mind of a person can do and think. It also teaches you about apology, and growth, and penance, and shame. As another individual in some industry was found out, I thought of these things, and I haven't stopped thinking about them, and I think of the image of Christ having been pulled down from the cross, where he's laid down, and the skin around his wounds is purpling, and his humanity is there. I think too of the image of Christ in a jar of a man's urine, of this figure warped and made to answer the thoughts of anyone who might approach it. I think of Ian Curtis. I think of Frances Sokolov. I think even of Louis Althusser. There they are. Seated. What have they done? What else have they done? My first bad novel was called *The Persistence of Crows*. I hate that it was published, but I also have to accept that it was, even to own it a little. I am full of mistakes.

IN THE TIME
WHEN MY MEMORY
FIXATED ON THE DEATH OF
PRINCESS DIANA

*My head is against the scalding yellow wall, my toes have torn my
socks, I eat something that's coming apart. I keep a light in case of
tremor. I use a boarding pass to mark my place. As for we who love to
be astonished, we close our eyes so as to remain for a little while longer
within the realm of the imaginary, the mind, so as to avoid having to
recognize our utter separateness from each other, a separateness that
is instantly recognizable in your familiar face.*
"My Life in the Nineties," Lyn Hejinian

17.

I forget the exact details, but it went something like this: someone interested in the difference between art and entertainment turned on some Beethoven as loud as it would go, and asked the listeners if they were entertained. Something on that order anyway. I do think there are complicating factors. I don't look at images of Gunter Brus to feel entertained exactly. I don't read about John Duncan's work or listen to Atrax Morgue because I want to escape exactly. And in turn I don't believe I seek this sort of work because I'm a particularly sick person. The violence and horror in the world committed by apparently average individuals leads me to believe that there might not even be such a thing as a particularly sick person. And when I open the pages of Sade, I'm not caught up in some sort of reverie, and when I'm watching certain apparently vile films I'm not in a state of pure bliss. I think these encounters are, however, a form of entertainment, the same as when I snuck behind a house at the end of a cul-de-sac one night, in Father's neighborhood, and walked in darkness to the top of a large hill there, and climbed a deer stand in a tall tree and looked down at the city below. It was entertainment and it was experience, and I did need it. The more like that you do, though, the less you need to sit with your face in a book. And the more you do have your face in a book, the less you need to compulsively masturbate and have a sad cum, as all cums are inevitably sad cums. I'm drawn then to the figure of an artist who is at odds with the world, and doesn't try to mend that distance or break from it but rather sits contentedly out on their little homemade island, sending back the occasional record of what they've been doing out there, beside the world.

18.

The watch Father died with is a silver Tissot that frequently pops off my wrist because of the design of the clasps. The battery on the watch is dead and the only local jeweler I've gone to was recently shuttered so for now I'm stuck in the small town in Idaho where we live, where we were when we heard about Father's death, with a broken watch. It was sent back with his effects and an autopsy written in Greek. I enjoy having the watch nearby and I enjoy not knowing much about the watch because the watch's value is sort of all its own and it could be from Walmart or worth ten thousand dollars and I wouldn't be aware. I wouldn't care. I like things this way. When I was younger I liked to spend time in the basement of my parents' house. Father had an office down there and we stayed out of it. He used the bathroom down there in the mornings and none of us used it. I remember playing video games on a small TV with my brother and my sister and a variation of our friends. When the death of Princess Diana happened I remember watching coverage about it on TV with Mother. Mother was attached to something Princess Diana represented and all I remember is feeling like it mattered. I remember scenes of people in mourning. This was my first real introduction to the end of the twentieth century. I believe the massacre at Columbine High School was the second. I was nine years old.

19.

The difference between guilt and shame is that we deserve it. Whenever I feel shame, it seems clear that I deserve it. The medicine I'm on, the therapies I've done, they try to alleviate these feelings using misdirection, and sometimes it works and even makes sense, but I still cling to shame. If art can only conjure a mood, I would hope to conjure an art of shame, a shame to be shared between two failures of the moral order. When my father died I was thinking about this kind of thing constantly. I spoke to several consecutive therapists about it. I spoke with my wife about it, all the things I felt ashamed of, and she finally had to shut me up—I wouldn't stop talking, I had a seemingly insatiable appetite for confession, which is probably why I always loved AA and NA meetings but hated working with sponsors. A room full of fresh faces is always going to forgive your shameful ramblings far easier than the same sad person you've been talking to for weeks. Even now, I feel compelled to apologize to you, and hope to be forgiven. I would welcome your apologies, for anything, and I would forgive you.

20.

I have it, the filth, the nausea, the paranoia, the readiness, the thoughts, the wetness, the dampness, the putridity, the saturation, the passivity, the violence, the criminal, the disgust, the sickness, the damnation, the water, the leaking, the urine, the excrement, the garbage, the vileness, the trash, the self, the wandering, the gasoline, the kerosene, the mud, the muck, the oil, the coarseness, the bodies, the blood, the light, the steps, the melting, the dead animals, the cannibals, the ugliness, the piss, the spit, the cum, every moment, I have it, the eyes, the organs, the liver, the jaundiced body, the yellowed skin, the burnt flesh, the wars, the body, the bodies, the murders, the corpses, the self, the mirror, the looking into one's own eyes, the filth, the scum, the rot, the compost, the nausea, the disgust, the sickness, the horror, I have it, all of it, every drop, there within me, and I am looking at the world, and I am weary at the state of it, and I am whispering somewhere hidden, a language I don't understand, and repeating it, over and over again, until the morning cuts my stomach open.

21.

Someone picked us up. I would've liked to arrive home and see people I knew, and feel calm with one another. I would've liked to see Father's face. I would've liked for my anxiety to vanish. I would've liked to be better all that time we were home to my wife, and my kids. I was moody. I was angry. I didn't understand why I couldn't just be sad, and quiet. I didn't understand why my reaction to everything seemed so wrong. I would've liked to meet Mother there getting off the plane. I would've liked for her to see my children and for us to reunite in a brief, sad embrace in the parking garage before we drove home. Things never work out how you want them to, not ever. You're consistently anxious about how things are going to happen so that when they finally do you're inevitably let down and depressed. This is the situation and it never stops. Life is always letting all of us down. There is the work, it is in front of you, and you must return to it, as he returned to it. As the citizens returned to the city after they'd watched it burn up all the disease spreading madly. The burning forests in California. The smell of fire as you walk out to take the garbage out on a warm Monday evening in Moscow, Idaho, your family getting ready for bed inside. The forests are burning as they were the night you arrived in the place. Ascending a mountain on a tiny road and to the left up on the mountain fire was racing down and time was moving and your wife-to-be was asleep and you would arrive and you would assemble the sleeping-bag bed and you would shop at the Dollar Tree for months and things would get no closer to making sense but you would persist and maybe that was sufficient.

22.

When we were in the car driving home it was Father's car and my sister's friend was driving and my kids were in the backseat with my wife and we talked about religion and a creek by the friend's house and drove in periods of silence and I remember feeling happy to be going back to Father's house then, and not thinking too much about how sad everything was. I had a message from Father on my phone that I wouldn't delete until much later and it was nice knowing it was there. We hugged and kissed our family members when we got home and I think some people—maybe distant relatives—were visiting to help out and give us food and things and it was good to finally see everybody. My wife was wonderful about asking how I was doing. I have a tendency to go silent when lots of people are around. I've never dealt well with crowds. Something in me shuts down and I can't find a way out of it. Even in the car heading back I clammed up. I just wanted to be home. My wife would look at me, and we'd roll our eyes, or we'd text each other, and it helped. Marriage, when it's best, is that ongoing huddle between two similarly-plighted friends, in love and making fun of people.

23.

The summer before Father died we'd driven to Glacier to meet my parents for some vacation days. This would be our last real trip with him. We brought the disc that contained my son's MRI results after he'd had some seizures and it was clear he was having trouble. Shortly after being born my son had contracted meningitis. Then seizures came and partial blindness came and favoring one side came and it felt like it was never going to stop—I lived in denial then. I was always trying to deny the reality. I still try to deny the reality. I tried to reject the idea that anything was going on with our son because nothing unexpected had happened with our daughter, and my relationship to our son felt largely the same. It turned out he'd had a stroke in utero, causing part of his brain to shut down, and after all settled it was clear he had cerebral palsy, and I probably struggle even now to remain aware of that fact, no matter how many times these moments repeat in my skull. My son is one of my only male friends, and even then when he was a baby going through all these things I tried to just be present because I wasn't sure how to deal with anything. At the time we were acquainted with a lot of different new parents, and several were facing very dire situations, and I've tried to remain aware of that, even if sometimes it doesn't do a thing. I just want them safe and happy. That's all I want. If they're able to experience that then I'm OK.

24.

Getting home felt like a small step in an arduous walk that wouldn't be resolved for some time. I was relieved to be free of teaching for a bit, but it didn't help matters much. We were miserable. People kept randomly weeping and needing to be talked to. My children were passed around as little beacons of warmth and hope, especially for Mother. Father's siblings were making their way to us. Whether or not somebody's there doesn't matter if you've spent enough time with them in a particular place. It's like the dreams I have about my father still. Being at his house, then, and being surrounded by these people who wanted to communicate and wanted to commune on the occasion of his death made him as present as ever, even as I felt this growing void. I think the void, though, was disconnected from his actual former presence in life, so that the two things exist forever simultaneously and neither cancels out the other. He's there. I'm not. Father died those days. Or maybe yesterday, I don't know.

25.

It felt good to be able to say fuck you to every living and dead thing in the universe because Father wasn't there anymore. Fuck you to Elvis Presley. Fuck you to the rest areas on highways. Fuck you to phones. Fuck you to writing, to art. Fuck you to speech. Fuck you to every billionaire. Fuck you to Bono. Fuck you to hospitals. Fuck you to my Luvox. Fuck you to my Seroquel. Fuck you to my insulin. Fuck you to waking up. Fuck you to every job that every person's ever worked. Fuck you to water. Fuck you to the right. Fuck you to the left. Fuck you to the center. Fuck you to New York City. Fuck you to California. Fuck you to my kitchen. Fuck you to Greece. Fuck you to shoes. Fuck you to reading. Fuck you to listening. Fuck you to everyone. Fuck you to cars. Fuck you to every insurance company. Fuck you to music. Fuck you to pants. Fuck you to sex. Fuck you to Freud. Fuck you to Gilles Deleuze. Fuck you to money. Fuck you to sleep. Fuck you to Joyce. Fuck you to coffee. Fuck you to tea. Fuck you to instruments. Fuck you to medicine. Fuck you to everything ancient. Fuck you to Proust. Fuck you to poems. Fuck you to chicken. Fuck you to eyes. Fuck you to healing. Fuck you to dying. Fuck you to this sentence. Fuck you to this sentence. Fuck you to this sentence. Fuck you to this sentence. Fuck you to this sentence. Fuck you to this sentence. Fuck you to this sentence. Fuck you to this sentence.

26.

We had been sitting in the basement on this leather furniture my parents had purchased that I would constantly get stuck to after laying down too long watching TV or falling asleep. I believe we saw it on the news but my parents had already known and told us what happened. Our babysitter, a nice college student with long curly hair, who had stayed with us while my parents went to Russia, had died. I believe she died in a car accident. I believe she was the one who stayed with us while my parents went to Russia, though I'm not sure. My parents went to Russia for about a month, to adopt two young boys. Adoption, at that point in the 1990s, was in vogue. Another family had adopted a Chinese boy. Another family my parents were closer with had adopted a Russian boy. A few months before this my parents sat us all down to say they were getting a divorce, I think—in retrospect I'm not certain this happened, and yet the memory is there. I believe my older brother was barely over ten at that point, if that, and all of us kids cried so much that my parents decided they couldn't get a divorce. Then came the plan about adoption, and I'm not sure how clearly related they were to my parents at the time, but whatever the case I think they were doing their best—it's very difficult for me to differentiate between things I'm certain happened, and thoughts, or dreams, or tricks my mind plays on me. Father worked a lot, and Mother was prone to depression and anxiety. Father's sexuality wasn't brought up to us until later, when they would finally get divorced, and so, for the time being, they were going to Russia, and we were staying back for a month with our babysitter, who would eventually tragically die. I remember, perhaps because I was about six years old, a powerful closeness to this babysitter. I remember being excited to come home from school and have her there. I remember giving her hugs. She attended the university in the town where I'm from and she was impossibly mature and cool. My parents had given her small things to give to us each day that they were in Russia. They were there for a month. I can't remember any of the things they gave to us but I do remember sitting around with the babysitter and watching things, or eating, or reading something. People talk about the change in America after 9/11. I don't remember that change. I remember, though, how it felt to have a babysitter you were close with, and this sense of their life as fundamentally tied to yours, and this admiration you had for them which often blurred with a sense of awe or attraction to their beauty. When I was that age I remember hearing about Hitler. I don't remember who told me. I always had this fear that Hitler would come to our house and take me away. I remember once when it was night and a babysitter was at our house and I woke up having been severely troubled by a dream about Hitler. I remember my babysitter wearing a yellow sweater from the university she was attending. After she passed away, a friend of hers became our babysitter, and they were similar. She came to Father's funeral, to Father's home to visit with us, and I remember briefly feeling as young as I'd been when I'd known her. Both of them had this warmth that I can't explain. I remember watching Disney movies in the evening after spending the day with friends swimming, or rollerblading, or playing video games, or something else. I remember sitting on the porch of Father's house where they had this massive TV lined with wood that had a vinyl screen. It was probably 1998, maybe 1999. I remember that comfort and it's how I felt toward the babysitter who eventually tragically died. This too is all blurred with the death of Princess Diana, the same relationship to the television and this overwhelming sense of tragedy, met with the closeness of my family then.

27.

I remember the meetings after Father died. I don't know when we found out how he died. It was strange being back at his home knowing he wasn't going to walk through the door again. I felt bad having people take care of our kids or leaving my wife with them when I talked with my family about his funeral. The thing that nobody tells you is that death is like everything else in life. If you're an anxious, stressed-out person, experiencing death is going to be like that. People try and push back against this sort of thing by having impulsive sex or getting drunk, but when everything settles back and they've got to look at the situation they're faced with, it's going to feel like everything else has felt in their lives—this constant presence of a dull and inexpressible ache, this pain. I don't know what medication I was on when Father died. I remember his siblings coming to our house and playing games together and talking. I remember all of us sitting around the TV watching something or playing video games. It wasn't really nice though. It was calm, and it wasn't bad, but it didn't feel like anything. People asked me things and I said whatever you say back to people who have asked you things. I never learned how to just talk. I'm always lying and always indirect and I haven't even stayed with a therapist long enough to tell them that. Father died on September 11, 2018, I think. I might have the year wrong. I stopped noticing things like that after our first daughter was born, and now I'm basically brain dead.

28.

I would have you know the work and engage it and when you're finished with it I would have you take it, all of it, and put it over the drain in the shower. Pack all of the pages of the work you've assembled over time on top of there in a sleek little mass, covers and pages of text or images bleeding through. Then, do something you don't intend to tell anybody else about, take a spray paint can and paint over the front of your body. Randomly but remain within the area of your flesh that will be covered by a shirt and pants. It's sticky and uncomfortable. The paint is thick. It's up to you whether to cover your genitalia. I did because I think it's sensible to spend a day or more with this secret thing happening under your clothing that you're not going to tell anybody about. Then turn on the shower. The ways the books are shaped and distinct will leave some room, ideally enough, for water to drain so that your shower doesn't just suddenly overflow. Stand on top of the work that is there, this work, and slowly knead your feet into it, letting the cold or burning hot water spray the paint on your flesh and fall into the floor you've assembled there on top of all this text. This is the relationship you should have with yourself and with the work. An author is there, with you, and would prefer this sort of treatment anyhow. Take time and let this develop as it needs to. Turn out the light. Sit down on the mass and try to distinguish between the texts and images you've got there. Call it your shame, and hold the experience close to your heart forever.

29.

I remember my babysitter being one of my first experiences with death and I also remember the death of Princess Diana. At the time I didn't understand it. I didn't understand Mother's desire to watch TV constantly after 9/11 had happened either. I was staying home faking sick and I changed the channel. Looking back, though, I think her processing of Diana's death must've come from a place deep within her, the teenager who watched with her parents and eight brothers and sisters when JFK was shot. The only thing that could really be done then was to pay close attention. To watch the TV and communicate with those people you see every day and try to move forward in this situation that feels impossible. That level of fear isn't something people get much experience with. If they do, if say they live in a third-world country being constantly bombed by other countries, if say they work in an emergency room in south Chicago and don't get through a shift without removing bullets from a stranger's guts, if say they're a woman in Juarez, Mexico, if say they're a woman on planet earth, if say they're a child on planet earth, if say they're in a stretch of aggressive methamphetamine addiction living on a reservation in Minnesota, if say they're on the run, if say their father violates them, if say they're schizophrenic, if say they drive a bus, if say they're a working mother, if they do, if their daily life is this way, if they see it, and they live in fear, and they witness new depths of fear each day, there are ways of coping that the world as such passes judgment upon, none of them really adequate to deal with anything at all, and each opening up new caves within the chest that hold no light.

.

30.

When I was young before I would've really had the words for it I called my anxiety a discomfort. There's a level of anxiety wherein every moment seems vaguely connected to an electrical socket reverberating a dull wave of constant paranoia and that's the kind of anxiety I've always had. I was first medicated for ADHD because that was in vogue in the 90s. That medicine made my weight plummet and my interest also and then I was hospitalized. We watched videos recorded by my third-grade teacher before and after I was in the hospital and it made us all laugh, my family and I. I was skinny and mumbling in the first, and jovial and average-looking in the second, separated by the month of outpatient treatment in Rochester, at Mayo. We laughed I think because the only alternative would've been to read into it and wallow a little. I didn't want to do that and I didn't want my family to do that and so we laughed. I don't think it's bad. In fact I think it *is* bad if you're incapable of laughing at the previous self. People are ridiculous. Being human is unbearably stupid. The second you stop being able to laugh at what an idiot you've been might indicate something dangerous. The anxiety, though, or discomfort, has always been there. In fact, laughing helps the anxiety. I don't need to drink coffee. I don't really need to smoke or anything like that. Sometimes I want to but it's not worth it. If I have coffee my anxiety is simply worse, and I'm twice as awake as I already was by way of my anxiety. As an addict there's often a temptation to find the end-all-be-all cure for my condition but it doesn't exist. Just like the ideal scenario in which to write. Or something in the past we regret or want to return to. None of it is real, and life is about acknowledging that when you're faced with it.

31.

I remember my life in the 1990s and I lived in Wisconsin and the parents were drinking Miller Genuine Draft and we were in the backyard and I was a creep. I remember my life in the 1990s and Columbine. I remember my life in the 1990s and Wendy's. I remember my life in the 1990s and the yellow school bus and giving notes to girls and never getting a note back, a little void there. I remember my life in the 1990s and the rooms at my elementary school and the bathrooms where I felt safest. I remember my life in the 1990s and watching professional wrestling and feeling whole. I remember my life in the 1990s and Ritalin. I remember my life in the 1990s and LA Gear. I remember my life in the 1990s and my neighborhood. I remember my life in the 1990s and going to the movies. I remember my life in the 1990s and VHS tapes. I remember my life in the 1990s and Grunge. I remember my life in the 1990s and *Behind the Music*. I remember my life in the 1990s and constant television. I remember my life in the 1990s and complete hysteria gripping everything. I remember my life in the 1990s and Y2K. I remember my life in the 1990s and moments on screens, video cameras. I remember my life in the 1990s and Pizza Hut. I remember my life in the 1990s and drinking soda. I remember my life in the 1990s and the haircuts. I remember my life in the 1990s and sleeping in. I remember my life in the 1990s and a sense of completeness, and my family, and the moonlight, and once Father, brought home drunk from a neighborhood party, carried up the steps and old voices are telling me what to do and I don't get it.

32.

This friend once, I don't know why the two of us were at his school. He lived in a part of town that meant he went to a different high school. Before that we had been very close. I don't know if both of us were addicts. I know that I was. We were curious, though, and we liked escaping stuff together. He was a nice person, probably the nicer of the two of us. I was sort of an asshole. I liked to escape stuff. I liked to leave the world and I didn't do all that well in the daytime. I went to a high school whose colors were purple. He went to a high school whose colors were blue. We were at his high school in its large gym watching people play basketball, I think. There were people there we knew and we always liked being in the stands with people. We were good at being funny in those situations. I don't think we were high when we got there, but we were trying to get high. We would've taken anything. That was something that bound us. I don't want to tell you his name. My name is Grant Maierhofer, I can't imagine it matters. I sort of had a girlfriend at the time but I was a very fucked-up person in a lot of ways I wasn't prepared to really think about too much. That's where the drugs came in. I think I was fourteen or fifteen years old. He was older than me and had his license. He smoked Camels. We would drive around a lot, with all sorts of people. We had gone there I think to find drugs. That was the hope, anyway. It was daytime. The way we talked, the way we interacted with the people around us, the way we joked even, it was clear we weren't really fitting in with them. In good moments we didn't really want to fit in with them, but sort of hover up above them, removed. This day, though, was strange. The middle of the day, watching sports that we didn't care about. One of our friends was obsessive about basketball. I envied him that, I remember. We went to a gas station then and bought a box of Benadryl and he took half and I took half and we went back to the school to watch some more and then we drove around smoking cigarettes until later when we went to Mother's house and I fell asleep in the basement in the middle of the afternoon and didn't wake up until much later when my friend had gone and I was very confused. I remember going upstairs and there was a bottle of antidepressants I hadn't taken for a long time so I took a handful of them and they didn't do anything to me but it was something. They were blue. Stout little blue tablets I poured into my palm. I think I found a bottle of gin or I took some other pills or I drank some leftover beers I had in my room that were warm. After I'd consumed this stuff I took a long shower and then I remembered that it was the day of my brother's graduation party. He was a couple of years older than me. I don't know if this was before or after I relapsed the first time. I can't keep things organized all that well in retrospect. I remember I went to the graduation party and I sat by the keg that was full of root beer and I pulled the hose for the beer keg over to me and drank awhile there. I think I took some clothes off and jumped into the pool. This wasn't the sort of party where people jumped partially clothed into the pool. Our family was there. All these people were there and I did this impossibly stupid thing. I looked like a gigantic fucking asshole. I can't believe what a moron I've been.

33.

I can remember feeling as though the end was always looming, and so I did what I could to ensure it never came. I only went to sleep when I was so fucked up it was impossible to do anything else. I only took time for myself if it was to fulfill some other addictive thing, to masturbate or take drugs on my own, to drink or watch TV. I was always looking for the feeling of being absolutely immersed in a stretch of being fucked up. In the morning when my mom drove me to school I would go into the gas station and buy a bottle of water, some gum or something, and a box of twenty Nyquil liquigels. I'd take them all before school. I never fell asleep from those. Benadryl was stronger and made everything feel much stranger, like there was speed mixed in. Closer to Sudafed, to meth. Nyquil just sort of took the edge off of things. I was always trying. I look at the world now and I see that everyone is always doing some version of what I did. I'm even doing it, writing this way. I do it when I watch TV. I do it when I eat. I do it when I take medicine. I don't take too much anymore. When I was using I might just take a random sampling of anything they'd put me on. I remember when I was younger, nearer to Mother, watching the TV as tragedies ensued in the 90s I could feel the edges of days and the sorrow that broke through there. Mother and I have always hated Sundays.

The only time they were anything was when something exciting could happen and you could sort of melt into the week without thinking. Otherwise there was always sorrow there. It wasn't drugs until I first took any at eleven years old and from then on that's all it was. It was films, or food, or drinks, or moments, or situations that I clung to back then, watching Mother watching the TV.

34.

I'm only really interested in the sort of writing undertaken by people apparently equally capable of a profound hatred that can sometimes exist in the heart of someone at the end of their rope. Falling down. I stand alone. I will never forget the color of the light outside the window in the room where I was hospitalized for depression and whatever else when I was seven. The wound started there. It was a gift given to me by parents who were confused and doing the best they could because it gave me access to that place below the tar of self and ego that wells up in the heart and allows an individual to escape life at need and separate from the mindless nodding dogs lining the street. Oh please. You feel this way but then there's something empty there. The assumption of this emptiness in their heads winds up doing less for you than fantasizing their thoughts. The anger in the face of a cashier. The fury in the hands of a waiter. The suicidal thoughts of a bus driver. I want to hold onto that. I want to hold onto the hatred I feel within when I stare at the sorry state of structures in the world as it stands. I want to go to the beach and lay there in the sun until it's freezing in the dead of night. I want to wade into the water with my pockets lined with rocks. I want to pick up a large rock and walk slowly into the water and just before my head's submerged I want to lift the rock high up and drop it right on the top of my head and collapse slowly into the moving water there, the little cloud of my blood and brain matter billowing out, softly. I haven't found a lot of peace. I've worked to find peace and I'm usually only met with a short reprieve from a day of anxious thinking. When I was young I would take drugs. Me and my friend would take any drugs that were put in front of us. We would go to secondhand stores and spend the day trying on clothes while we were very stoned on painkillers and whatever concoctions a gas station offered. This is for him.

35.

I do not wake up and feel the necessity of work. Beside my bed there are typically a number of books from which I've read fifteen pages or so. When I was a kid I did not keep books around me. I started to write in a rehab center, or before that, in the hospital, or something. I don't remember when I started to see things a certain way. I would always obsess, fixate. When my parents got divorced my OCD became more pronounced. I would move my fingers and fidget in sequences of five. I was medicated for a time then. I might've had it before. I've had doctors since then wonder whether it was tied in with my alcoholism. That's the biggest problem with addiction. The longer you're able to stay clean the more your brain wonders whether you were ever really an addict at all. You've got to find ways to remind yourself. OCD helps, oddly enough. I can see how extreme those thoughts are and the feelings therein and I realize that if I were to take a drink, or if I were to use drugs, I would need such a syrupy quiet to coat my brain that I wouldn't stop until I was a corpse, and even then I'd probably haunt the living over it. I remember being an emotional kid. I remember looking down at my desk and wondering why I didn't seem to feel like the kids around me. I remember being in first grade, and second grade, and third grade, and moving from classroom to classroom until it was all done and I went to an alternative school to test out of high school after I got sober for the last time. Once Mother went away. Twice maybe. Once her depression had so overwhelmed her that she needed to seek hospitalization, help. Another time I don't know where she went. She might've been visiting my younger brother. We had this felt material at home. I realized that I could make her a simple vest to wear using the felt, and so that's what I worked on in the basement while watching TV for most of the day. I gave it to her at the end of the day and like most mothers she was kind and supportive of this thing I'd done. I'd never done anything like that before and I haven't done anything like that since. I don't understand why I did it.

36.

I was a little fucked-up kid and prone to lots of inward hatred even then. I hated school. I hated waking up in the morning. I hated my family. I hated nearly everything except television. I still hate most things. I spend most of my life trapped in my skull. My skull hates me. I hate my skull. I hate to think. I hate music. I hate recovery. I hate the AA meetings. I hate walking. I hate getting fatter every day. I hate the anger I put out into the world. I hate that my kids may know me as a middling loser. I hate that I'm so fed up. I hate America. I hate everywhere else. I hate to read. I hate to learn. I hate to see the world again. I hate sitting down to write. I hate my phone. I hate the people. I hate the street. I hate church. I hate art. I hate the artists. I hate the music. I hate the city. I hate Idaho. I hate the world. I hate the president. I hate the internet. I hate their talking. I hate my body. I hate my legs. I hate my gender. I hate my face. I hate my race. I hate the bicyclists. I hate the runners. I hate the meatheads. I hate the anorexics. I hate the actors. I hate the writers. I hate the antiseptics. I hate the writers. I hate the image. I hate Twitter. I hate speech. I hate the forest. I hate the snow. I hate the wars. I hate the films. I hate the conversations. I hate the classrooms. I hate the talking. I hate the spinning world. I hate the sun. I hate the straights. I hate the liberals. I hate the conservatives.

I hate the days. I hate the stores. I hate the countries. I hate the books. I hate their piling up. I hate their opinions. I hate my fat gut. I hate the masturbation. I hate the showers. I hate the cars. I hate the windows. I hate the workers. I hate the rich. I hate the organizations. I hate the fraternities. I hate art.

37.

I remember taking a shower downstairs and trying to meditate on thoughts of my own death. I thought of taking a rifle and putting it up under my chin sitting there in the shower and spraying my brain and blood up along the white wall for someone to come and see. I thought of going out and buying a bottle of vodka and sitting in the car taking pill after pill until things started to get blurry and then laying my seat back to ensure I choked on my own puke. I thought of going to the lake where someone had killed himself and doing it in the same way, paddling way out into the center of the water, having a cigarette or something, then jumping in and swimming as far down as I could until I choked, the taste of acid and vomit and muddy water my last experience. I thought of going over to these highway bridges by Father's home and walking up and toward an incoming semi on the side of the road, jumping out into the middle when it was close enough and being spattered and crushed by the massive machine. I tried to breathe very heavily there and take the thoughts completely in and expel them fully when I breathed out, adding a new means of dying where that one left off in the bath over and over and turning the water hotter and hotter until an hour had passed and my wife was knocking at the door, confused by what was happening. These are not points of pride. I feel ashamed, stupid.

38.

When I was a kid I remember being inside my own head in situations where I was inside my own head later in life as well. For instance, it was rare that I would have a session with a counselor or therapist whom I did not envision having sex with. As life went on it became clear that I could envision this with male and female therapists alike. The America of the present moment seems most interested in what people have to say if they aren't just average white heterosexual people, and for a time I emphasized my bisexuality because of that—I'm not straight but I'm boring in other ways—but it's also a thing that was basically always there, as well as the occasional feeling of gender dysphoria wherein I see a woman and imagine being her because of the way she seems to so comfortably exist in the world. I remember farther into the past when I really felt the need to explore whatever sexual leanings I seemed to have, so I'd go online and talk with men and talk with them over the phone and it became clear then that this too was part of me. Older men mostly, I'm not sure why that was. I think I tried to explore it in *Postures* but I bet I failed there too. The title says more than the book ever could. I'm an opportunist dilletante little shit. I remember coming out to certain people. I'm keeping to myself. The thing always is to keep to yourself. What would you hope to know about me, given that I believe in privacy? *What do you know about me, given that I believe in secrecy?* Who said that? Gilles Deleuze said it. He said *if I stick where I am, if I don't travel around, like anyone else I make my inner journeys that I can only measure by my emotions, and express very obliquely and circuitously in what I write.* He said other things. He jumped from the window of a building when he was old and an illness was unbearable. He had no fingerprints. His fingernails were kept long because of it, or something pained there. My own perversion seemed to materialize in tandem with my treatment for whatever ailments I seemed to have in my brain. It started with the therapists though. First the one at my elementary school when I was seven or eight, who I'd imagine having sex with while we talked about my thoughts and I frequently lost my lines of thinking because of it. It's rare that I'll be in a situation with just one person where I don't think about sexual things. It's a problem. I'm sick to death of it. *What do you know about me, given that I believe in secrecy?*

IN THE TIME
OF PATERNITY AND THE
VOLVO 240 WAGON

*I believe Proust has been overly esthetisized, aseptisized. I would
like to return his aggressive thrust to him, to restore his violence. His
"Jeunes filles en fleurs" are in effect "Fleurs du Mal."*
"The Place of the Madeleine: Writing and Phantasy in Proust,"
Serge Doubrovsky

39.

I had a habit of staring at other men and women and obsessing mildly about becoming them. They were often thinner people, thinner at least than I. They'd often have paler features, darker hair or clothing. They looked a certain way, fixed, and something about them drew me in. I struggled to explain it. It seemed curious to want to become someone with a different genetic makeup than yourself, or at least a different physical one. I couldn't explain. I read about individuals who were trans, say, and it didn't quite register as the same thing in my head. I saw, I thought, a person's essence, and preferred it to my own, and believed there were changes I might make that could eventually result in a shift in my fundament that would make me feel complete. I also think that these concerns never really revealed themselves in other circumstances because I never kept anybody around me long enough to address it. When I lived in Chicago I sort of experimented. I spoke with older men and settled into a sort of frustrated bisexuality that I'm still processing and experiencing on a daily basis. I tried to embrace my draw toward becoming various women by allowing myself to become emaciated, eating stuff only bought at the Dollar Tree, mostly candy, and smoking a lot of cigarettes and masturbating multiple times a day so that the pleasure center in my brain was more concerned with that stuff than with the comfort provided by a large meal. I wrote *Postures* in that place. I let my hair grow. I let my beard grow. There's a femininity to letting your beard grow a little wild that I don't think enough people really appreciate. Melville said *it had always been one of the lesser ambitions of Pierre, to sport a flowing beard, which he deemed the most noble corporeal badge of the man, not to speak of the illustrious author.* Find a picture of a man with a large beard with flowers in it, for instance, and it becomes pretty clear. Or Oliver Sacks. His beard was always something I greatly admired, and I think it spoke to the fluidity with which he was able to embody the patients he wrote about as well as to his eventual discussion of his sexuality. I went to see films all the time, alone. I wore uncomfortable leather shoes that I'd buy at secondhand shops that had a small heel to them and I'd take my writing classes and my other classes and I'd write about things and I'd try to figure things out and I'd go for long walks late into the night where I'd see people exchanging sex for money and there was something beautiful about those months and years I spent there.

40.

This in turn meant I purchased too many clothes. I purchased too many pants that were similar. I purchased too many shirts with slight, only slight, variations between them. I purchased too many pairs of black boots, or shoes, or tennis shoes, always black. I had all of these in an office that was overfilled with stuff. I had too many books in there that I never read. I sat in there idly thinking and scrolling. I sat in the office thinking about other writers or artists and watching videos of them. I'd see someone there and feel myself pulled toward them. I sat on this uncomfortable leather chair which gave pain to my tailbone and I looked at videos of people accomplishing things and I'd stop and fixate on a person in the background of one of these videos, a looming presence, and I'd fixate on becoming that person, or taking them into myself, their entirety into the whole of me. I hadn't asked doctors about this. I'd asked doctors about things mostly related to happiness. I didn't necessarily think this sort of thing was the kind of thing which might be medicated away to create more happiness. I thought of things like intrusive thoughts and suicidal thoughts as the kinds of things which might be medicated away to create happiness. I thought of days when I felt like I'd rather just stay in bed as things which might be medicated away to create happiness. This, though, didn't seem like the kind of thing for which I could be prescribed medication which in turn might create happiness.

41.

Going to the store was a nightmare. Going to work was a nightmare. I'd see the way someone's jeans fit and immediately have the sense that my clothing was completely fucked up and wrong. I'd watch somebody getting into their car and the way the wind grabbed their hair at just the right moment to create something novel and I'd go into the bathroom and stare at my own hair knowing how inept and fucking stupid it was. I would start to talk to my wife about these things and she was always good about knowing where I probably needed to stop. She would be good about finding something funny to it, or saying something outrageous that set me right again. Once when I was walking into a store she randomly opened the door and yelled CAN YOU GET ME SOME VAGINA CREAM?! and I fell in love with her there all over again. It was so funny. It was so insane. I like to kiss my wife, to hold her and sometimes to dance a little. For all my mental rot and roiling I can be very traditional. I'm lucky, and I'm a cliché, sure.

42.

I would give anything to have Father back. I would give anything to have hugged him that night before he went off to bed. I have never been very good at expressing myself in a manner that makes sense. I get sad and become obsessive, or mad and become indirect and quiet. Father came with my little brother to stay with my family in Idaho. They stayed the week and I was anxious most of the time. I said goodbye and I felt myself closing up in sorrow. At the door it was clear he was sad and I was brief and didn't say much of anything at all. We went inside and my wife couldn't understand my reaction, and then I sat down on the couch and started to cry. I felt broken in half to have Father and my brother leaving for the Midwest. I would have my wife and my children but being there with my family I felt opened up. I wish I'd simply cried in Father's embrace, but my wiring is shot. I wept on the couch and felt so much pain. I miss him every day in some manner or other. Life is impossibly complicated, and I don't think it's stopped being impossibly complicated, and I think that is marriage, and parenthood, and a career, and all of it. You can't wallow in any mood too much about it. Even writing it here feels rotten and I'm torn between blacking it out or removing it.

43.

This was the first time I'd really considered finally buying a 1990s Volvo 240 Wagon. I had hassled my wife too about wanting to wear a dress or to exclusively wear vintage sorts of perfume. I'm not sure. I'm not sure about the political climate. I think that things had grown progressively more racist then, perhaps, and it was on everybody's mind, and nobody was responding to it all that well. Everything was falling apart constantly through the years in which all of these disparate things were happening and we were trying to make sense of it. I took more medication, believing it might bring happiness, where in the past I just took drugs and spent days on end looking at videos on my phone made by people in little quiet rooms either doing horrific things or talking about the ways in which the world was being manipulated by a cabal of some racistly caricatured ethnic group. This was a low point in time. I became obsessed with that car because it seemed like the perfect machine. I never understood men who wanted to buy cars that needed fixing up. I'm mediocre at most basic tasks. It's an issue for me too. I wish I could simply go out and accomplish something complex under the hood of a car but I cannot. I try. I do my best like anybody. The Volvo 240, though, gave me a sense of comfort because I'd seen them driven by certain people over the course of my life and I became very obsessed with the idea of having one of my own that I could work on and engage with for a prolonged period of time. I started to keep public domain images of them with me. I wanted to have one to drive for the rest of my life.

44.

Another time, I think because I wanted to try and force myself to shut up for several weeks to get some work done, I set fire to a coal and I opened my mouth as wide as I could. The coal was made for grilling. They're coated in something that makes them catch fire easily. I was in my backyard and as far as I could see everybody around had gone to bed. My wife had gone to bed. My children were asleep. The dog was running around between my legs. I had the coal in tongs and I held it until I could see bits of orange shining through the black. I'd wanted to do this for weeks. When I wanted to do something—something like this—it always started in thoughts and they came up whenever something was wrong. With my pinky I was feeling depressed and sitting in Father's basement and I remembered the saw he had. Ryobi. Bright green. I helped him remove some staining on his fence for a couple of days before that and eventually I found myself in his basement there, a piece of wood in front of me, the saw turned on and rotating, and I shoved my pinky into the blade along with the wood and felt it cut clean through the meat of me. After I cut the finger off I covered it in cloth and went to the bathroom to flush the remainder of my pinky so that reattachment would be impossible. I took a long cold shower and felt the pain of it and slowed the bleeding. I was able to go about my days for a good while before anybody noticed. My wife saw it eventually and I admitted that I'd cut it off on purpose one day a while back. It wasn't infected, thankfully, and I promised her I wouldn't do this sort of thing again. I remembered staring, years before, at the blurred male on the cover of *Jernigan*, and the moment when he shoots himself in the hand. I'd opened a collection of stories called *Marcel* with that moment as an epigraph. I've always been drawn to people taking something out on their body. For a long time I dreamt of it. I wanted to do it. I had wanted to do it. I wrote another book called *Clog* about a murderer who's determined to murder himself, cutting off his limbs with a saw in a shed and burying them in the surrounding forest. I don't know why I'm telling you this. I hope it isn't an ego thing. That's all I can hope for. I like it when human beings take whatever violence the majority of humanity projects out into the world and direct it inward. Not suicide, not really, but this long slow process of fighting with oneself, remaining at odds with oneself, at war with oneself. That's what's important to me, I think. Then, so, the thought came of the coal, this violently hot object making its way down to my gut, removing the hatred that I felt existed there. I would look at the profiles of people I hated on the internet and stoke this anger, and feel disconnected from the world, and want to do something about it. My response, then, was never to feel violent toward another. I would always get violent toward myself. I knew that I was the problem, that my hatred was the problem, my jealousy the problem. Knowing this, I fantasized the object opening my throat and blistering the skin of my open mouth in the cold night. I opened my mouth and the cold world entered in as I lifted the object up and felt its warmth at the edges of my lips. I saw the orange of it and I opened up and lifted the tongs until I mustered the energy and separated the tongs with my other hand and the coal dropped into my waiting mouth. It burned me at first and it felt like a quick shot of cold. I must have passed out because I awoke on the ground with the coal burning the outside of my cheek and I hadn't screamed much or made too much noise because nobody had come outside but the feeling that was in my throat was like I'd swallowed a burning cup of tar and it tasted like I'd inhaled a massive gasp of nasty chemicals and held it after the burn. The outside of my cheek on the ground was already blistering and I crawled over to the hose and ran the water over my open mouth and face for what must've been half an hour. I didn't stop until I could mumble without a heap of pain. I lay out there crying until the sun came up, cold and shivering.

45.

Back in a house filled with people and everything was happening right in front of me and all of it was slowed and I don't think I accepted then the death of the man. He had been such a large presence in my life. I had lived such a puny little life. I don't know if I wanted to accept it. As always, since the kids were born, I wanted to go somewhere alone and sleep for a month, then come back and deal with every problem. You get a minor dose of it each night. They sleep. You use your phone until you can't open your eyes anymore, and then you sleep.

46.

When I was younger I used to say I was going to die when I was twenty-one and I wouldn't have read a book. I didn't fully understand that until more recently. I understood the death thing. I would take any drug put in front of me. I would drink anything put in front of me. I became a type one diabetic when I was ten and I've never been very good about taking care of myself. I really didn't care if I died when I was twenty-one. Most days when I wasn't on something I was thinking so much and so destructively that it's a miracle I never killed myself. I still have those thoughts. I take a lot of medication. The book thing, though, only became clear more recently. I liked Darby Crash, a mess of a person who did not seem as though he read much. Lately I'm very uninterested in reading all over again. It's not from a hatred of reading, I just can't see the point. Other things are easier to get lost in, and that's something I value. If I experience aesthetic pleasure it's usually more in catharsis, an occasional scream that literature's never been great at providing. Sometimes, though. The large editions of de Sade that Grove used to put out. These massive mass market paperbacks filled with his writings and others' critical writings about him. It was easy to get lost in those in a long bath, reading about sex and god and nature and darkness. If I'd known when young that this sort of reading existed I might've discovered it quicker. Even then, though, I can take or leave it. I don't know that it matters and I don't know that I'll ever know. I don't know where entertainment stops and art begins. They are similar, they are even quite possibly the same. I have no real position on the matter. I just think you should be honest about your interests and spend your life doing the things that bring you that sort of joy that holds no guilt. Do what you can to remove guilt from things. Open yourself up to your own interests and trust them. Find something in the world. It's there. There is a world inside the world. I'm asleep.

47.

Why would I write? Why would I write about it? Why would I write about my life? Why would I sit down and write something today? Why would anybody sit down and write anything these days? Why wouldn't I just go for a walk? Why wouldn't I just pee on someone's car? Why wouldn't I just have sex? Why wouldn't I just put on a song? Why wouldn't I just punch a hole in someone's car? Why wouldn't I just fight a stranger? Why wouldn't I just lace up my boots? Why wouldn't I leave earth? Why would I stay? Why wouldn't I just find ten more writers to despise? Why wouldn't I unearth their secrets? Why wouldn't I read *Kill List*? Why wouldn't I escape? Why wouldn't I lay on the ample belly of Francis Ford Coppola? Why wouldn't I hug the dog? Why wouldn't I give my wife a kiss? Why would I write a thing? Why would I share the work? Why would I engage the internet? Why can't I just leave? Why can't I get my own cow? Why can't I get a big cow and name her Jolene? Why can't I fix everything? Why can't I cushion my children from this stupid world? Why would I read? Why would I read a novel? Why would I listen to a podcast? Why would I vote? Why wouldn't I go for a swim? Why wouldn't I move to Iraq? Why wouldn't I collect Norman Mailer's hair? Why would I read the *New Yorker*? Why would I respond to the world?

Why would I focus on anything? Why would I try? Why wouldn't I put on the boots my sister got me? Why wouldn't I wear some sweatpants every day? Why wouldn't I listen to some music? Why wouldn't I listen to the Sonics? Why wouldn't I save some pictures to my phone? Why would I teach a class? Why would I get some degrees? Why would I study? Why would I endeavor? Why would I write a book? Why would I write another book? Why wouldn't I be stuck in the 90s? Why couldn't I drink some Kick? Why couldn't I get a slice of pizza? Why couldn't I listen to Joy Division? Why wouldn't they cancel me? Why can't I be dead? Why can't I take my medicine? Why do I take my insulin? Why do I paint? Why do I write? Why wouldn't I write? Why would I write? Why should I write? Why wouldn't I sleep? Why wouldn't I just eat a bullet? Why wouldn't I watch the television? Why wouldn't I follow sports? Why wouldn't I invest my money? Why wouldn't I have friends? Why wouldn't I take a shower? Why wouldn't I get counseling? Why wouldn't I watch pornography? Why wouldn't I eat a cheesecake? Why wouldn't I stare out the window? Why wouldn't I get my pilot's license? Why wouldn't I try and eat my car? Why wouldn't I develop an unhealthy, illegal obsession? Why wouldn't I go to prison? Why wouldn't I join the military? Why wouldn't I become a prostitute? Why wouldn't I fight the air? Why wouldn't I play music? Why wouldn't I watch a film? Why wouldn't I go to sleep? Why wouldn't I become a professional wrestler? Why wouldn't I be a janitor? Why wouldn't I have some kids? Why wouldn't I grow up? Why wouldn't I make some coffee? Why wouldn't I trust the directors of films? Why wouldn't I trust the directors of art museums? Why wouldn't I go for a walk? Why wouldn't I take more antidepressants? Why wouldn't I nurture my fear? Why wouldn't I hold my fear? Why wouldn't I walk? Why wouldn't I burn myself? Why wouldn't I set myself on fire? Why wouldn't I go to the monastery? Why wouldn't I be there in the morning? Why wouldn't I mourn?

48.

For a long time the daydreams I had about my death took place in hotel rooms I'd been inside of that I fantasized about when I thought I was probably nearing the end of my time on earth, sometimes the room first, a vague sense of anxiety and wanting to escape it, sometimes the rope first, the bullet, the pills. I tried to incorporate this into the death meditations then and found it was easy to lay back into these narratives about my death like easing into warm water. I was trying to use them practically. I was trying to use them to engage my past and future and to really dwell deeply in the mood there, the feeling there. I'd imagine going somewhere to buy some drugs, somewhere else for some alcohol, somewhere else for some sort of tobacco or nicotine. I'd come back to the place and lay on the bed closest to the bathroom wall. Maybe I'd take a shower and masturbate and turn on the television and start to drink, taking a pill or two and continuing in this manner until I reached a deep lateness in the night. I'd walk outside then, barefoot, and wander around the city for a couple of hours, eating more drugs and taking drinks and hiding from the world. I'd stand there watching the people. I'd think about Father's last night and the massive hall where we'd held his funeral ceremony where my former friend's mother sang "Danny Boy" in a strange falsetto and my sister and brother read things they'd written and Mother sat next to me crying and I didn't read anything. I'd written something and it was included in the program for the funeral. I talked to these people from various stages in Father's life and I ate food. I held my daughter or my son. I can't remember the order when all of these things occurred. I can never keep things exactly right. I want to but I can't. I try to but ever since I was twenty-four or so my memory has been a series of vague electric twitches and long waves of anxiety rather than something clear and readable. The best the idle thoughts of death would bring me was some sense of stability that I was nearing a definite turning point, even if it was the end. I read about figures in ancient civilizations who knelt as their throats were cut, or their bodies shot through with hundreds of arrows, then lit on fire and sent out on a slab of wood to die on the water. I read about the famous suicides, and histories of suicide, that attempted to put this thing into some kind of context, but there's only more. A false perception of clarity soon gave way to more and more narrative.

49.

I think I was drawn to Yukio Mishima because of his physicality. His death. Even now, the first thing I think about is his death, his body. It's probably because he wasn't straight, but married. Had a child. Believed in an ideology and made art. Participated in the final destruction of himself. His emaciated form in a government building bleeding out, communing with the corpse of Pasolini on the ground, murdered by his own car. A farmer in the city. *Do I hear twenty-one, twenty-one, twenty-one?* Mishima as Saint Sebastian. Father as Saint Sebastian. Myself as Saint Sebastian. I carry his picture still. I had seen versions of death before. I kept the picture Man Ray took of Marcel Proust on his deathbed in my office. My grandmother had died and I still remembered the plasticky way she looked at her funeral, surprisingly small for someone who cast an immense figure in her life. The early pictures of Proust, youthful with a mustache, French, hair a bit shiny. The image of his death looks completely different. He's got a beard and his hair is grown out a bit, and he's laying there like a saint. In the older version of me there is a slew of disappointments that I have watched my entire life. I have watched myself fuck up all things. I have never stopped watching myself fuck up all things. My writing. My family. My marriage. My body. My health. My mind. My medication. My addiction. My alcoholism. My world. My war. My diabetes. My heart. My work. My talking. My trying. My teaching. My children. My dog. My family. My eyesight. My diet. My water intake. My experience. My happiness. My depression. My anxiety. My fear. My obsession. I try to fixate only on little totems along the way. The looming voice of Scott Walker, louder now that he's dead. The simple Volvo 240 Wagon. The watch Father wore. The boots my sister bought me. My wedding ring. These stabilize, help me to remember. These put me in a right place.

IN THE TIME
OF DEATH

Don't worry you'll get over it
You'll grow up, you'll calm down
Another youth, another fashion
You'll get over it, you'll calm down
"No," Subhumans

50.

There's a picture of Flann O'Brien I keep on my computer. There aren't many photos of him available so it's relatively easy to find and is I think the most circulated photo of Flann O'Brien. His teeth don't look that well, and he's bald, and the hair that remains on the sides of his head looks greasy. I saved it because to me the picture held a sort of beauty, I guess when considering the context of his works. I told this to someone, a translator, and he said that O'Brien looked pretty torn up by alcoholism. He's wearing a tie. I think it's true that he does look torn up by alcoholism. I still feel a lot of beauty when I look at the image, though. He looks like he lived the life his work defined. His work didn't define his life, though maybe it did. He looked like he was involved in everything he did, perhaps to an unhealthy degree, and maybe he needs some coffee and a shower, some weeks of rest, but I see a powerful beauty there, not even knowing much about the man. I wish I did. Maybe someday I will. I've got to finish some work before I'll have the time. I'm always putting things off. My sense is that he was deeply immersed in his work, and that it was strange, Joycean work, but there was also some restraint with him, perhaps like Beckett, and drinking, and life, and misery, and all of it consumed him as it consumed the work, but the work remained, and even he remained for as long as he could, and you can sort of read that from the image, glean this understanding. Sometimes having a picture of someone like that, before taking in the whole of their work, before fully understanding what they did, can take you farther into what they accomplished than the other way around. I find it's far more educational to attempt and take in certain artists' physicality, and the picture moves me still.

51.

Since publishing a bad novel I'd been lucky to publish some other mediocre writing. When I say these things I'm not fishing, and I'm not being dramatic. It's impossible, unless you're an egomaniac— and many important artists are—to consistently feel good about your work, and if you do, and you aren't an egomaniac, there are probably questions you should ask yourself. I also attended a university for an MFA in creative writing—which (the MFA generally) is an economy created by writers who have needed to figure money out aside from writing, and which is as fraught with ugliness and possibility as any economy. I've asked myself a lot of questions about what writing is, especially fiction writing, and the sort of writing that I'm interested in. I frequently feel very hopeless about it. Some writers I know are lucky enough to make good money from just writing, and they don't seem to feel as hopeless as the rest of us. I teach basic writing courses and technical writing courses to make ends meet. My books haven't made me enough money to live by any metric, and they likely never will. Many writers with large audiences are frequently quoted about writing and its importance. Their sense of its importance seems always to be guided by independent wealth, or money from the writing they're doing, and what's more they almost never seem to realize this—they just think they're geniuses whose every thought ought to be heard when it comes to the economy they've successfully maneuvered to their benefit. I really question the importance of this stuff, though, and I'm often at a loss. One writer said *literature is entertainment or it is nothing.* Another said *I'm a writer, not a reader.* These are the mindsets I'm usually faced with. The two paths for the novel in my mind, with the novel serving as a stand-in for all writing, because sure. It might be entertainment, but I think this would mean that entertainment is far more complicated and beautiful than we've been led to believe. I might be a writer first, a reader second, or third, or fourth, or fifth, but even still this means that I am concerned with whatever it is people are able to do within this artificial space. Once more recently I sat in the bathroom of a local co-op on the toilet reading the early pages of *Death in Venice,* and then reading a bit about the life of Thomas Mann. I've heard that book talked about for much of my life by various people. Probably first on television, and then in various educational institutions I found myself in. Then later when a writer was talking in an art museum in Minneapolis about the film *Stalker,* which I'd seen screened there a few days prior. It was always just referred to as a great book. This thing that we should receive as passive readers or something. *Stalker,* too, a work of genius that it was our problem to navigate. Sitting there though, briefly cool from the summer heat, reading and reading about *Death in Venice,* of Thomas Mann as a father, as a husband, who also found himself terribly outside of his moment, because of his obsessions, everything was different—I felt that I needed to ingest the text because it spoke to things in myself that felt off. I've never been in Mann's exact position, or shared the content of his obsessions, but I've never felt particularly straight or content within such a model. It doesn't matter, not much anyway. To witness that vulnerability, though, is something I've always responded to. Sometimes I think the critics have failed, or that academics have failed, to properly champion the work of writers as wonderful feats of vulnerability and humanity. For me these two—and more heavily vulnerability—are the true mark of worthwhile art. Instead there's focus on esoteric ideas by chain-smoking French philosophers whose work often reads like a bad *Finnegans Wake,* and is so incomprehensible that the likelihood of two academics or students or people reading the work and then communicating about it similarly is just impossible. I don't know what the work is for.

52.

I relate then to the obsession of this person, this patriarch, the constant thought of this patriarch. Perhaps he's in the mountains, writing there while his family mills about. Perhaps he's clucking like a chicken and making his wife laugh. Perhaps he's sitting in a wheelchair at the edge of a city square and a boy is walking through, someone he's able to identify with but someone elusive. Perhaps he's making mistakes, or a single, large mistake. He's failed. He's a failure, somehow. He's Pierre. He's Thomas. He's Pierrot. He's Ferdinand. He's Fred. He's Marcel. He's May. He's Arturo. He's Adam. He's Kathy. He's Chris. He's Scott. He's Zelda. He's Eddie. He's Ishmael. He's Stephen. He's quiet. He's breathing. He's Anne Imhof. He's Anne Imhof's friends. He's Greg. He's Charlotte. He's Serge. He's quiet. He's planning. He's weeping. He's off there in the corner hid. He's hiding. He's Gertrude. He's Alice. He's the little table on which the manuscript began to pile up—slowly, slowly—he's the table where a sewing machine is bound up, a chance encounter between items which articulate some purity. He's there, right there, and you can all see him. It's a hot day, perhaps in Berlin, just before the war. The sun burns through everything, even thoughts. Perhaps it's Vienna. Perhaps it's in a classroom and a man is standing on a chair, showing his ass to a crowd of shocked viewers. Perhaps he's painted his face stark white, with a black line down the center that's still dripping. Perhaps he's being excommunicated from a church, some church, but in turn from his family. Perhaps he'd written something that pushed so far beyond what they thought acceptable. Perhaps he was a little queer. Perhaps he loved women, but the company of a man, a large father, drew him in. Perhaps he'd die. Perhaps he's dead. Say he's dead, there, on the ground, for everyone to see. A farmer in the city. Wilting into the dirt because he misunderstood a situation. Beaten by homophobes in the night in Italy. Beaten to death. Run over by his own car. Perhaps they'd heard of his film. They hadn't. Perhaps they had. Perhaps the film was screened. Later people would try to justify it through politics. It doesn't fully work. It can't fully work. How could something like this work? Nothing like his *Trilogy of Life*, those playful films. An extremity that can't be justified. A Cain's book. A roman à clef. A story of a vile husband, a patriarch, playing chess with taped-together syringes. His hair long. He's gained weight. Perhaps that's him. Perhaps he's there.

53.

I scrambled to get a suit for the funeral and overpaid. Things were over surprisingly quickly so I scrambled to return to the store and return the suit that afternoon. We had a meeting at Mother's house that she'd only recently moved into. She would be returning to Father's home now that he was dead. That house holds a unique magic for those of us who've lived there, it would've been a shame to sell it. I remember the long days of my youth with friends or by myself getting into all sorts of things throughout the place. It was probably too large. I've always loved horror films about big sprawling houses. That fear feeds into the magic of the place. As much as my youth was spent driving around doing drugs and going to other people's houses and drinking and fucking around, it's all still bound up in that house, this space that serves to represent the life and the city within it, it's all piled in together in every brick of the place. I remember going out late at night to get stoned and laying there on the ground with my friends, making each other laugh and staring up at the immense northern sky. I remember fucking around with girls all over the house, and the one boy I'd ever done anything with in the basement and Father's hot tub. I remember when my sister had small pigs as pets and we'd chase them around the yard at night. I remember the various times I had tons of essential strangers over for a party or something and I drank so much that I wound up walking around with a knife or threatening my friends or lying to Mother or picking a fight with a stranger or cheating on my girlfriend. The good and the immense ceaseless bad and all the shameful moments bound up together. The little red lines of Ambien I managed never to overdose on. The Hydrocodone my friend stole from his grandmother that we drove around eating for months. None of it ever ended and every ugly bit of it is stuck to the sick part of my heart.

54.

One way that things could've gone or did go for me—before the
real marriage and before the stability and before I'd found some
way of making sense of things, before Florida and before Idaho
and that—say I had stayed in various communities and learned a
bit about sustaining myself through alternate means. The women
in a sort of village beside an underpass in Pennsylvania had taken
to calling me a dog. I'd added the rest later after my reading of
whatever the manuscript became, but it was in that village I took
on what's become the set of problems I'm now devoted to. I didn't
so much flee my situation as I was plucked from it, but nonetheless there was guilt. I have unwelcome thoughts. Day after day I
experience unwelcome thoughts, intrusions. It got so that I was
convinced I was near to murdering or violating the people near
to me and because of this I confessed to a counselor who chose
whether I'd receive assistance, and it was he who spoke with the
authorities. If there has been any small gift in what's transpired
it's my changed relationship to thinking. When I was in the old
home then, a different life, I'd stumble around the children I'd been
helping to raise and the thoughts might overwhelm me for weeks
at a time. These weren't my children and I might've just as well
been alone. This wasn't my life. My thoughts about the present

and about the past and about whatever future I might reach were just as likely to be conjured up against me, in opposition to me, actively fighting whatever me I might've had there. I might find myself consumed with sin for hours until I'd have to speak about it and my partner encouraged me to try confession because the pills weren't working. I'd confess and then need the priest to assure me he wouldn't be calling the authorities and I'd confess all of this to my partner while she slept next to me. The medicine allowed me to sleep. I don't know which medicine I was on then in this version of me that never was, it just became more listed shit within the manuscript I'd had some part in putting together. That's about the end of it. Once I took it I could not stay awake, and this was good for a person like me. The authorities came some days later and I was brought in for questioning and because I was in the room I talked to them more candidly than even my priest—whoever they were, whichever assemblage—and thus I was plucked from my circumstance and put into one of counseling and recovery and court-mandated living and I would not be able to see those I loved for some time. I would always be watched and monitored, and this was based on thoughts, nobody was ever interested in accusing me of anything. They just knew it seemed impossible I could fit into that circumstance again. This was the sea of my past living. The lives I did live or could've lived, it didn't matter. Even now if I open myself up to thinking, if I look back, in any direction, I'm just as likely to be shown false information, stuff remembered because my brain wants me to drink, to go and steal some drugs, to hide away somewhere. To live beneath a bridge, anything. These moments weren't my living but they were in my stupid skull nonetheless so I piled them into the stupid manuscript the stupid text because they're just as much a part of me as my own memories, and my brain has never made distinction, faulty and pathetic and rotten and soaked as it is.

55.

Because of this then I accepted things. I didn't try to fight anyone
on anything then and when you're against the courts this means
you'll soon be in a circumstance deemed adequate by people who
have no interest in the quality of your days. I accepted this, too, as
a sort of punishment for the sprawl of my thoughts and the problems in my head. I had murdered in my head and ruined lives in my
head and been a horrible person in my head. Whatever words you
say to the world during those lines of thought it's unlikely you'll
feel at peace by any light thereafter. This was the worm of living,
the little nagging thing that each of us has tacked to our pineal
gland by a rusty nail that gives us full and unbearable awareness
thereafter, pus and infection there. I accepted it, then, and these
events slowly led to my circumstance living in a village of those like
me beside an underpass in Pennsylvania, near to the town where
I thought my paternal grandmother had lived, but I never found
her. I've never lived in Pennsylvania. This didn't happen. I wasted
my life. The lucky ones had tents, the rest of them slept in packs
under wool blankets after the drink took them for the night. They
burned small fires and fished in the water below and occasionally
someone might earn some money and bring back a large jug of
cheap vodka and a loaf of old bread. Sometimes we'd get lots of

champagne yeast and mix up massive tubs of juice with it. They'd eat these things and speak and sing and the days and nights would blur together like this surrounded by all those trees and the long bridges and the high gray sky poked through with sun and they felt calm. This was a world I could've lived in, and it was thus like any other world in which I've lived, and there were people I was meeting and I was a character in their world and I was writing them into my own, into this ill-shapen manuscript, and looking up at the sky like that afternoon in a hammock on the farm in Minnesota and I could say out to the world that I had wasted my life, and it was the extreme of me, the rot of me, the outward burst of anger in hatred of me, pushing through to the world in long lazy yawns while I drank and needed sobriety, and all terrified me and when I was able I left to run back to the world to be of the world. This is the world inside of the world. I fell in love with the world in the dirt there and spent my days laying back floating in the water and wasting them, every minute wasting them. Another stretch of wasted years before some purpose. Did I relapse then? Was I a teenager then? Was this before the book, the manuscript? Was this before Chicago? Was this before the world? Situate it perhaps a bit for us. Find the place to focus on and the family you'd left and the counselors you'd talked to. Someone I'd left a long time ago. She had her life and kids. I was young. It was time for me to flee, to find the work. Stop telling yourself these stories.

56.

This proved just a step on the way when suddenly I decided to leave behind this region of the country entirely to find something then completely new. This meant movement south from where I'd been and eventually this found me crossing into Florida, writing about it then and the sun beaming down brightly on a small car I'd borrowed. I had always wanted to live in a place where the sun was constant. I'd told this once to a professor of writing in a class I took of his that was on fiction writing and censorship. There was an older man in the class who looked like he'd had a very hard life, his skin was aged. We were supposed to write on writers who dealt with censorship and he wrote on Peter Sotos, and eventually had Sotos communicate with the class, and Sotos in turn used it in his book *Mine*, a book that I was too scared to have around after I'd had kids, it seemed criminal just to own it. When Sotos communicated with the class it didn't go well, they wanted him out, they wanted to quiet his talk. Sotos used it in a book and I had given over the will of my months to this depressive anxious tendency then, older then, and spent my days walking around and told my professors I wouldn't make it back and I stopped attending school the second spring in a row and before I'd left I'd written something in the class about my desire to be in the sun, to eat fish and simply exist in the sun. Back then, then, in Florida, in the past, then, I had made an attempt, and it had failed like everything.

57.

A version of me had left after Pennsylvania and after the small collapse and had traveled to Florida where I lived and existed primarily through stealing with a girl who called herself Flamingo—I never got another name. Her father had sent her a bit of money for housing and this was enough along with minor capers which allowed the two of us to eat and drink. I could not afford insulin and thus kept primarily to proteins and water, and visited a local free clinic when I could to receive injections and the occasional pen, and typically a languorous afternoon of monitored blood sugars before returning home to Flamingo, where we'd lie naked on the floor with the window open and a stolen fan bringing the evening's cool air over our bodies and we'd escape. I don't remember what we talked about there on the floor. I remember this primitive state we were in. I sang "My Love Is Like a Red Red Rose," I remember. We walked around singing the songs from *Quadrophenia*. We walked around singing in Ian Curtis's voice. We walked around Florida smoking in the bright lights and drinking what we could and I don't remember if this was before or after the first relapse or when but I remember the feeling there of being lost in the sun and knowing that my family might want to hear from me but I wanted a minute more, I wanted to cement myself into the corner of a beach there and just have a minute more with Flamingo in the light. This is where my particular version of obsessive-compulsive disorder plays into things. I am comfortable saying that certain things have happened in my life, and even with those I'd still wind up a little anxious after the fact for imposing certitude on certain things and thus it's best to just avoid removing any cards from what's assembled there on the floor. People have memories. People write autobiographies. People verify that certain things have happened in their lives. Because of this particular sickness, it's best for me to go forward a little unquestioningly. As a supposed inventor of narratives through language, in turn, there's no shortage of trouble. I'm getting those shocks again. When I type for a bit, I get these shocks. My fingers slap the keyboard and I often type some nonsense there. It just happened, just now. I'm trying to work on it. It's called harm OCD, where you'll still have fixations and obsessions with checking, with numbers, with repetitions, but there's this added dimension of fixating on horrific stuff, and a lack of certainty regarding this stuff, and this feeling that you might've done things that don't align a bit with what you seem to feel you'd do in your real life, ever. The way that someone sitting at a job interview might idly chance upon a thought of shooting the interviewer, because maybe they'd seen it in a film somewhere, or maybe they're angry, and then it'll go away. With me, it doesn't go away, and what's more it's not a little daydream but a sort of criminalized certainty that I'd done something horrific, that this was a near certainty, and that this was the most important thing for me to figure out because I probably belonged in prison. This, then, too, went into the manuscript.

58.

Our situation meant that neither of us could afford medication and this meant that I was prone to long stretches of a sleepy depression and Flamingo her wandering and screaming. I'd go to the free clinic for diabetes equipment but the people in there who'd talk about mental health issues usually became bound up in some sort of hospitalization, or put on some sort of list—we figured—and neither of us wanted that. She'd spend days hidden in movie theaters at times and I would curl into a ball and hold myself in the shower while the water went from boiling to cool and back to boiling over the course of hours and I'd masturbate intermittently to try to relax. I thought then of the life that I had lived and the things that I had done. I had behaved badly. I had treated people like shit. I never feel good looking at the past. I become convinced that prison is following me, slowly, patiently, and someday I'll be there. I think of this and the history of writers and artists and all the massive fuckups every human person commits, all the people we wrong, all the families we leave behind, all the relentless stupidity and selfishness. I do not believe that selfishness is a prerequisite for anything in this life. I do not believe that selfishness is a prerequisite for anything in this life. Mierle Laderman Ukeles. Mierle Laderman Ukeles. Mierle Laderman Ukeles. I think of her when I'm feeling this way. I remember lying down in Florida and Flamingo was gone and the old *Helter Skelter* movie came on and I realized my life was bound up in that and dragged along with that and I would be stuck under the thumb of that dumb murderous impulse for the rest of my life, this unrelenting stupidity, this humanity, human being. Missing Flamingo I would sit in the shower and she would be writing and I would be stuck in the world and I would piss in there and I would shit in there and I would take an X-Acto knife and cut my legs up in there and none of it quite made sense or helped me but I persisted. I'm a sick person. I guess I'm just a pretty sick person. I wasn't built right to be a person in the world. Stop making excuses. You've hurt people. I'm sorry. I am sorry and I think about my wrongdoings every single day. I'm sorry. At the end of long days like that finally we'd go and lay on the beach and drink from a bottle of orange juice we shared and smoke as the sun set and sometimes they'd even set off fireworks and I would feel OK again, to be there in the heat. Life slowed to a trickle out of a faucet on the side of our sun-scorched house and people there on the beach celebrating with their families and on vacations from the world and I could live in that for the remainder of my days and feel OK, but I felt shame. I still felt shame for leaving the world and running into the sand and leaving potential and possibility and the comfort and the security I had started to build up, and even the slips and all the stupid fuckups I'd made in life. I'd started to feel a pull to return and atone for who I'd been. I started and continued to put these things into the growing manuscript, shoving aspects of myself into previous aspects of myself until the thing got bulbous and water-logged.

59.

I would wake up some new place and be on the beach, say. I would watch the sun come up in the morning way off on the horizon and feel its warmth begin to comfort me as I sent messages on a stolen cell phone to strange men and women with whom I'd couple, myself alone or maybe Flamingo and I. I'd meet someone and take nude photos for their art project and then I'd rest. I would sleep in the bushes and wake up covered in grubs. I couldn't handle staying in one place for any length of time. I couldn't handle watching the morning fade to day. I could spend the long afternoons with Flamingo watching the people go by and we'd be drinking coffee laced with LSD or MDMA and the sun would burn us and at night we'd find some place brightly lit to couple. It was then I think that I started to write about Flamingo, though I can't be sure when it started. I don't know when things start and stop anymore. It's as if there are these things in my life that are constantly there and occasionally I'll let myself wade into them and I'll lift my head and suddenly everything's changed, I'm in a graduate program or I'm in third grade or I'm in rehab or I'm getting married in a hotel room in Wisconsin and everything is about to change, is changed. The day before my marriage I lay for an hour in a sensory deprivation tank, which was something I'd always dreamt of doing, any sort of space of silence, of meditation, or of extreme discomfort, forcing myself to look directly at myself and not flee, not rush to explain. I saw a photo once of John Cage walking through an anechoic chamber at some university, when I was editing my first book in Chicago, and I'd been obsessed with them ever since, with spaces like that. I tried to write a place that had them and say I was a journalist and wanted to write about the experience, but it still would've cost too much money. My wife knew I'd wanted to do something like this, and so set it up for the day before our marriage and it was a nice moment in my life. I've never been to an anechoic chamber, but that hour or so the day before my wedding was truly peaceful. I showered before in a shower with glass walls. I lay there and focused on a small red light. Afterward I got out and showered again in the shower with glass walls. I could feel the change happening, this move to being married, and for all my idiocy it felt peaceful, and I looked forward to my life with Kelsey, and with my effort to not be a selfish asshole, that desire has only grown. For a lot of writers the notion of marrying, of having children, of working a steady job, is somehow antithetical to their work. I don't want to read the work of people who have removed every aspect of life from their lives in order to work.

60.

I found myself later married to the person who had saved me, a child on the way, and attending a university nine hours from Utah's Great Salt Lake where Robert Smithson had constructed his *Spiral Jetty*. I thought endlessly about the rampant changes in my psyche and circumstance and felt myself at war with a deep, fundamental pessimism. The notion of bringing a child into a world so besotted and reeking with rot and abuse horrified me. The notion of existing past my twenties horrified me. The notion of marriage horrified me. I had failed in everything in my life up until that point. My twenties were a swirl of mistakes that I kept revisiting and reliving and I was sure I would somehow ruin this and I was waiting for it to happen any moment. I would take my work and feed it through systems, computerized systems that would alter it and turn it against me, create a ruined literature that severed my naïve youthful intentions. I had written naïve, youthful things. I was now an aging, naïve failure. Then later I found myself married and attempting to make a life for myself and each day trying to be less of a despicable piece of shit. I found myself less interested in a literature with much humanity. I wanted everything computerized, broken, vile. After the first bad books then I published some of these books with the help of an architect who lived in Kansas and we both tried to support one another while it seemed that every other aspect of our lives was falling apart, but mostly that was me. I liked the image of Smithson slowly putting these materials together, piece by piece, until this large spiral emanating from the land got formed, and layering materials on every inch of that, and trying to ensure this thing wouldn't be killed by time, or weather, trying to create something that would outlive him and his children and on through generations, but using materials from the earth mostly, using things we all have access to, trying to do something that wasn't egotistical—anybody could stumble upon it and walk along it and hold onto images of it, it wasn't about the artist, he was secondary to the work in this rare case, where his humanity mattered far less than the object he'd succeeded in creating. This rare moment where that's the case, and it's the case with Ukeles, and with Acconci, and with Smithson, and it's something to aspire toward in writing, the removal of the human being.

61.

The subject is what, in this sort of thing? The subject is the living? The subject is the event? The subject is the language used? The subject is memory? The subject is one's own life? The subject is a little bug, caught in the ice of a flash-frozen lake? The subject is the individual's moods, through the vicissitudes of their pathetic life. The subject is what, exactly? And why? Where is the work positioning itself in the world, as an aesthetic matter? Perhaps we'd all like to go back to bed. The subject is a little living being on a little lucky rock. The subject is the way a morning can stretch out when your life isn't a pathetic careening between moments of abjection or regret. The subject is the white floor of the shower in the dark, discernible only because of the glint of light beneath the door. The subject is the death of the author's father, or the death of the author, or death. The subject is the way it felt to open every window in the small studio apartment in Minneapolis late at night and to lay on the floor there a corpse there and let the wind blow over your naked body as a CD played Fauré on the small player against the wall. The subject is fiction, a fictional subject, a subject stitched together from the sentences that pass through one's head as the father's death passes one year, then the next, and then a decade, and then more. The subject is as long as life. The subject is the mouth affixed to the ear and any communications therein, every stinking word. The subject is the stench of the individual and the warmth of a bottle of perfume purchased from a German woman who'd kept the bottle all through the war and saved it, a little heart-shaped bottle, encased, only to sell it to the author or the subject one morning one weekend for several hundred dollars. The subject is an old Buck knife. The subject is a caught fish. The subject is an antagonism between the self and the head it's protruding from.

62.

The two of us, that is Flamingo and that is me, had made our way to Cuba one weekend and we spent the entire time blind drunk and wandering around the strange and constant lights of the place. We were sleeping together then happily and with others and we lay down late the second day to rest alongside a fire as high as a truck around which various strangers were cooking sticks of chicken. We woke to the sudden cold of the night and made our way to a large white building and wandered inside to find more strangers dancing around a table and singing out the name of someone no longer there. We danced together and the face of America was no longer there and the ugliness of the morning was no longer there and that night we all sat in a large hot tub and felt the day's waste melt from our arms and legs as we became quiet and held to one another in the blinking glow of it and the world felt us and held us in a nest of humanity that hardly spoke but sang or danced as the lot of us were ushered into the bright light of morning when we could fall asleep on the busiest beach and wake to hundreds and thousands around us all thinking and feeling the same thing and welcoming the mess of it unto us as we stared into the sun and went to swim. As the orchestra played for the two of us we danced hand-in-hand along a beach outside Havana and sang along to one another. Our hands would break and one might spin a bit onto the dune and stumble as we made our way back and we'd hold one another close as the music of *Les Quatre Cents Coups* played out behind us and we were children in the lights and it was a profound thing we witnessed there. It didn't happen. We'd left behind the hatreds of our lives and the past work and had found something entirely new something to hold onto in one another something that the other recognized and it was profound and immediate and we fell laughing staring up at ten million stars as we burped and spat and knew we'd never have to return to the world and could exist in a perpetual state of return a sense of youth a sense of hope and everything would be OK if we persisted if we kept walking and living this way and welcoming the light it could all be OK. I had come from the Midwest. I had come from Pennsylvania and Flamingo had come from New York or somewhere else, she never said, perhaps a hospital—we'd both been intermittently hospital-ized, and seldom hinted at that. Flamingo's dead mother had the small home there where we could stay so long as we helped pay the remnants of an ancient mortgage and so every month or so she'd visit the bank and give what she could, whatever we'd assembled. We arrived back from Cuba on a burning day and I was wearing heavy boots covered in sand and muck and Flamingo wore black denim shorts pulled high and this ripped white T-shirt. That day we poured ourselves large cups of water and sat outside in a small pool holding one another in the sunlight as it burned the skin of us in a long, restful rotisserie. Flamingo's mother had a small televi-sion she'd bought at Walmart and one DVD and so that night we watched *Vertigo* in a tired stupor as the night extended out and we saw the neon of Miami out the window, exchanging a tray of ice we'd drag over our necks to cool down and eventually falling asleep on a couch with only a sheet when things finally cooled. There was the sense then of this stretch of my life needing to end, of needing to venture back and return to something, an honesty, a challenge. I felt this raw shame looking out the window and knowing all I'd done to wind up in such a situation. I tried to communicate to Flamingo that I needed to leave but that I would try to write what happened and the time then, the purgatory time, this breakage, was difficult and burnt.

63.

When traveling across the country I found myself lost and didn't care, moving but didn't care. Once I sat on the beach with hands in sand on a stretch of coast in Texas where the burning heat made everything seem sopped and impossible. I thought there of what I'd done and felt regret, felt shame, dug my hands deep enough to feel cold packed wet sand and looked out at the ocean and waited for my friend to return. My friend was any friend, perhaps Flamingo, or someone else. My friend was the friend I'd met and kissed and sat within a car staring at a burning parking lot while the friend's friends danced around in tattered black jeans hugging one another and embracing the end of days. These were my friends. They were my friends. I dug my hands deeper and laid myself back and felt miserable at all I had not managed to accomplish. I had written a bad novel and lucked into publishing it too soon and lucked into whatever else and fucked around with people who didn't care about me and sucked off old men who didn't want to talk and wandered streets and gotten dirty and felt the world caked onto me and miserable and all of it was rotting my insides out and I hated the book and I hated Texas and I needed to sleep for one year just one whole year. Everyone was bickering in the world and things were coming to an end. I could feel it. I could see it everywhere I went on the rank laps of old drivers I could see it on the couches of college students watching television sopped there as they were with all the heft of their minor histories and screens in their hands and I was fine with it, it didn't matter, the screens in their hands. It was OK. The world was OK, would be OK, nothing burning yet or falling apart yet or stormed or shot or reduced to animal violence. I had bought a Snickers bar and so ate it on the beach there having pulled a hand back into the heat I put the melted mass of it into my mouth and felt OK everything was OK. I took a sip from a glass-bottle Coke my friend had bought me. The two of us, later, lay in the sand in dark and pulled at one another's parts and the tide waded in slowly around us the denim our shirts the black fabric of all of it running through us and such as it was it wasn't so bad it was OK, we felt alright, to be alive then the two of us. A little midnight at the fringes of America as the remainder of the land was shifting putrid and gathering armaments for a seemingly endless slaughtering of everything and everyone forever. The tide was way in.

64.

I experienced great pangs of anxiety and threat in just about everything then, after the leaving, after the changes, after the new relationship and after the births of my children, the past and my past and the future and their future made everything fragile, and I was certain something would break, I was stuck in the past and things reacted accordingly: the world was made of potential dooms for me; my marriage would fall apart because of who I was, stupid things I'd said and done, the stench of the past to come back and ruin everything; my role as a parent meant that everything was tinged in plague, every single thought and act a threat not only to my life but the life of someone unaware of everything, unaware of all the putrid rot that made up this America and every minor misery waiting for the opportunity for whole destruction and full sleep. I should like for the work to be a little object for someone to pull with them wherever they're going, a little fragment of brain. A piece of that useless anxiety put to use in the little exchange. I've never been to Father's gravesite. I hope to go there soon. Life gets away from you. I left Flamingo somewhere and went home to the Midwest and I made my way out West where the highways sprawl out like long breaths of calm and the little place where I got my education was a little home for those years, as I fell in love with the world and started a family, as I became married for good and saw things grow simple in some ways, and immensely complicated and emotional in others. The classes were the same. We talked about the work, the ideas behind the work. I read a bit, and walked around. I liked the earth. I liked the words. I liked the music. I liked the people. A version of America. A life within America. A disgust within America and a fate within America.

65.

.

There was nothing to say. There was nothing to write. Things just
sort of happened and if I was lucky there was some sort of device
nearby which would entertain me. That's what the days had started
to amount to and maybe part of it made me sick. That's how disconnected a person might become from what they felt they ought
to be, that deep inner thing. I couldn't even say for certain whether
I was disgusted with myself and what I did. There was just a sus-
picion. It was likely, it was a possibility. And then there was the
aching in my mouth. Last year it had been on the left side, and
a dentist had removed a failed root canal with some bad growth
that had caused the whole thing, leaving a gap in my gum I was
constantly tonguing at. This year, through whatever hung rotting
within me, the pain had shifted to the right side of my mouth and
a certainty seemed to dawn that I'd lose my sibling tooth from the
other side to keep things in order. I feared I'd then wear my teeth
and my gums down. I remember this as one of the first small dra-
mas of my married life, the first time I was paying close attention
to the whens of my life and attempting to apply aggressive care to
my teeth and gums so as to avoid certain aging embarrassments. I
got gingivitis. I had the tooth replaced. Disease was spreading all
over the world. I had a cyst above my front teeth about the size of a

dime, and every new dentist I saw stopped to focus on this first for a time, then realized it was alright, but the rising and falling of that drama never altered the severity of the feeling, the mood. Gucci put out a video featuring an aging Kenneth Anger, his hair grown long and slicked back, like an emaciated Céline, and missing one or two teeth up front. I don't know why but I've always felt a little bound to him. Not the work as much as the person. I don't know why. It's just a feeling I have. I like to listen to Liszt.

66.

I've always got to consider how wrong I could be. There would be minor things, waking up and being certain it was Sunday based on how godawful everything felt. Thinking I had something to do when there was nothing to do. Thinking someone had said something some way when nothing was said. This was one of the large realizations of my adult life, coming into it, that you had to stop often and look at the ways everything was arranged, and consider just how wrong you could likely be about every single angle of it. The idea that a person can't stand the taste of something that someone else could sit devouring for hours. The idea that a song could make someone feel comforted, and engaged, and whole, while for someone else it could sound like a nuisance. I think first this was an aesthetic lesson, as well as one of love. When you love someone you're going to look for things that unite you. I think when you're getting older those things are less and less significant. You're a teenager and they don't like the same music you do, it won't work, it can't work. This seems so ludicrous when you think of the world fifty, eighty, a hundred years ago. Imagine leaving someone because they liked Bach and you didn't, or you liked the cello but they enjoyed the harpsichord. The twentieth century has been enormously detrimental to human consciousness. We're always looking for differences, picking grievances, opening and reopening wounds that separate us from others' slightly different, inaccessible wounds. There's nothing there, but we look for it anyway, we prod. I like, then, to sit and imagine how wrong my predilections could be, how wrong my leanings. I like to listen to music that annoys me. I like to read things that I have an initial aversion toward, or even better a shame about liking. I like TV shows that I disagree with. It's important. Writing, or making art, can be an incredibly alienating thing. You build this little island for yourself. You separate yourself from the world except for sustenance. You hone your interests and influences so that the work you make is indicative of that work, that appreciation. I believe you should return to the world. I believe you should always be there within the world. I believe that you should fall in love with the world, pay attention to the world, warm your hands over the world. Nobody really does an adequate job of telling you to pay attention. We just lean closer to those who seem to agree, who want similar things, who are satisfied by similar aesthetic experiences, but that's the mistake. You age a bit, and look at the past you, and you can realize it. The clothing you wore, the politics you embraced, the music you loved, if it continues through every decade of your life, you ought to ask yourself if you're opening your eyes enough to the world. Find out how you're wrong. Intimately imagine your own deaths, there, staged out in front of you to witness.

67.

A preoccupation it starts with me sitting at my computer while a television set plays in the background and on the computer's screen I'm looking at an image of what's supposed to be Mizutani. I'm never sure, though, and that's part of it, this sort of researching. The image shows a Japanese male, emaciated, with bangs and the rest of his hair about the length of the majority of the Ramones in their heyday, and there's a piece of technology in front of his face, probably a microphone, but it also might be a strange edge of a guitar and whatever it is that's the relationship I focused on when I looked at the image. Listening to a bootleg live recording from 1977. It's my favorite year. They play the usual stuff. Takashi Mizutani. Moriaki Wakabayashi. Their lives were violent and impossible. The hijacking of flight 351. More violence. More sounds. What matters is the relationship. A male, starving himself and wilting slightly but more in the manner of Prince where gender is shattered, a thousand mirrored pieces on the floor the world can bother itself to figure out. Leather. Metal. Strings. Noise. I'm captured by this moment, this interplay of power, this submission to the sound, this strength above the sound, only reached through the submission. I'm looking at the image again and becoming transfixed. That's all it is. I obsess with them and obsess with them and obsess with them. I want to look like them. I want to be them. I want to become them. It's comforting to think there's someone who only wanted to play something simple and loud and perhaps they had a hand in the bootlegs that have been released and they've had a hand in other ventures but for the most part they just wanted a loud scathing noise to throw back in the world's face and they weren't even posturing as if they were doing anything important outside of a block's radius. Artists can be unbearable when it comes to what they expect art to do for the world. People who grew up reading books convince themselves by the time they turn around to write them that books have an unbelievable effect on things. They don't. Art doesn't. It just isn't that important. The human GI tract is thousands of times more important, more interesting, and arguably more worth your time. Some artists seem to get that, and their work winds up feeling twice as vital because of it. This resignation. This submission. This failure. Perhaps this is Mizutani. He was one example of the sort of figure I would grow obsessed with the longer I was married and the longer my life persisted in the manner it did. I have always sought father and mother figures, father figures longer. Mizutani was one. His position as an artist and the clouding of things with the politics and violence. Again Mishima too, the life the art and the protest and the violence blurring it all. Resisting recording, resisting putting what you did live into something transferrable and compact. With age I've been drawn to these figures, those outside the world, just outside the world. They hover out and above it and the art they make from it is enlivening. It gives you purpose whether you want it to or not. It's there. I could sleep in that achievement.

68.

I don't have anything to say. I have nothing to say and so I'm saying it. It's in front of me, this ugly orb or something. The pink light that was outside of Dick's door. Horselover Fat. This looming sense of god. It is likely the amphetamines. How many amphetamines had I taken? They were all taking them. Everybody was taking them. America was taking them. Americans were taking them. Hitler swallowed bottles full. Sartre was on an insane amount of drugs. Pictures of him late in life are yellowed and pink and nasty. They would swallow a handful with their morning coffee. They would swallow a handful of barbiturates before their shower in the evening. There's nothing like that feeling. A wide stupor in the mouth. An opening of the gut unto the world. You should be talking to your wife. You should solve your problems. You should stop whining. You should apologize to every person you've ever met. Instead you're listening to the music, zoning out and writing out your thoughts this way. There's nothing to say. The manuscript has no place anymore, it's pulped and unreadable. There's no way out of this mindset. Ugly ugly ugly. I must not think bad thoughts. You should be picking me up. Instead you're dragging me down. They'll stone you. While you're driving in your car. They'll stone you. This is life. It's all a cliché. I'm a cliché. We can't escape it.

She saw it young and understood we are all living it out. How to escape it but the scream. We've got to scream about it. In our little homes. There's no way to escape being a human person. All your ugliness. Your stupid jokes. Your bigotry. It's all there, the ugly orb. Perhaps it is a VALIS, a system, a pink light outside your speeding door. Fucking asshole. Keep thinking this way and keep trying to think this way. You can't escape a thing. You are all a Nutella generation. Fucking asshole. Fucking nitwit. Fucking look at the way you speak, it's so goddamn offensive. Try again. Look at a different image instead of *Brian Jones Died For Your Sins*. Music from the death factory. Derek Jarman in his garden. Keep your secrets. An open work. Open plan living. A place to deposit your fat graying ass. Loser dipshit nitwit. Go away and sleep in hell. Bye. I don't have anything to say. I have nothing to say and I am saying it. Say you're sorry. The medium is your burden, your dignity. You're repeating yourself. You're a liar. You're asleep.

In the Time

of Grant Maierhofer,
Old and Sick

At age 49, she became gravely ill and died a few months later. As was the custom of the Poor Clares, she was buried without a coffin. She was exhumed 18 days later after visitors noticed a sweet smell coming from her grave and some experienced miracles. Her body was found to be flexible and uncorrupted. Six hundred years later, her body remains intact. Her skin has blackened from exposure to oil lamps and soot, but still she sits, clothed in her nun's robes, on a golden throne behind a glass case in the Church of the Saint in Bologna, resplendent in death as she would never have wanted to be in life.

"St. Catherine of Bologna, Patron Saint of the Arts," Loyola Press

69.

I don't know what they say about the future. They talk about the Jetsons. They write about cannibalism, about space. They write about the walls in caves, vacant spaces where people haven't been in centuries, only to find some touch that matches the contours of a tent village on Mars. I am living through that rot, or seeing it, projected out there for me to walk up and exit again, new. In another cave in my skull I can see the future as this complicated horrific block in the center of a large room looking down on me, telling me to submit, to change, to flee. I had taken my Seroquel and my Fluvoxamine but I had decided I was going to try and write something down. I hadn't done this in a very long time, not really, I don't know where the manuscript then was. I used to want to be a writer. I used to try and be successful at writing. Now, when I looked around, I wanted nothing to do with it. The words didn't matter. No matter how I arranged them, or what I did, I couldn't squeeze life out of it, not really. But something had started to feel different. The world had started to clarify a bit. I felt a strong sense of purpose and I think this sent me to the work. So I was sitting at the Brother typewriter I'd used to write things when younger. The clicking of the machine was relaxing me. I think my wife came home as I got started but I couldn't be sure. We hadn't seen our granddaughter then in a number of months. Whether she didn't want her family to see her or something more vile had happened we couldn't really be sure. We tried to find her. We tried to help our daughter. We asked what friends we had. We were always close with our grandchildren. They meant the world to us. We were determined to help our daughter. She was barely sleeping. She'd started drinking more. I'd contacted a number of private detectives to try and contact her. Nobody had much success. Some thought she'd somehow gotten to the Middle East. I couldn't be sure. My wife, because of it, was inconsolable. I wish I could say that this is why I hadn't written, but I'm not so sure. I think if anything I would've been more compelled to write under these circumstances, to make sense of her vanishing. I hadn't, though, been writing for a while before she'd gone away. The companies I worked for were easily calmed via emails and a bit of work here and there so there wasn't much to do with my days. I watched films and TV, or videos on the internet. I liked the sound of the machine though. Our granddaughter's name is Melody.

70.

I dug my fingers into the keys of the machine and felt them generate clacks of letters on a piece of paper I'd pulled from the floor. I wrote her name. I wrote *you have my undivided attention*. I wrote about my sister. I wrote about Ireland. I wrote what I could remember of the old Scott Walker songs. I started writing something about myself and where I found myself then as connected to this very fucked-up thing. The problem was we weren't sure if it was a very fucked up thing. She had done this sort of thing a lot. Since she was fourteen and she ran away to drink for a weekend with an old boyfriend. Since she was sixteen and she stole one of our daughter's cars and crashed it into a rest area hundreds of miles away from home. Since she was seventeen and ran away from treatment center after treatment center. Since she was nineteen and spent a month on drugs in Israel. Since she was twenty and got arrested in Brazil for stealing a car with a trunk full of drugs. Since our daughter had her live with us for a bit and she worked with me. She did these things. She reminded me of myself. She did these things and then she came home for months and her grandma and I would take her to movies and we'd go out for dinners and she'd find some sort of part-time work or maybe get back into school and we'd either hear from her or not. She'd return to her parents there, and we'd have a big dinner and an evening together trying to sort everything out. It happened. Time didn't really matter. I can't believe it's what I became. I have no idea if it's real. I hate it so much, not knowing. I hate seeing these things play out in any direction. And you, you ridiculous people. She'd been gone for weeks or months. She'd almost been married three times and each of them caused us no shortage of hell and stress. We were able to pay for things, it didn't matter. We were always helping out our kids. That didn't matter. We wanted them nearby. All of them. All the grandkids had stayed with us for stretches of time. My marriage has been through hell. Plenty of it my fault. Some of it not. The point though is none of us are unfamiliar with stress and feeling bad. Melody herself is capable of enduring an astounding amount of pain and confusion. I wrote about these things on the machine. My wife's name is Kelsey, I wrote. She's a wonderful grandmother and we're happy more often than not. I had a bottle of vodka I kept in my office and I went to the file cabinet to grab it and take a long slug. Nobody knew about it because I'd been very determined to have my place in that office be entirely my own. I don't remember what year this was, this later world. I don't remember things like that. I've taken in so many various forms of poison and the like that I couldn't keep track. I saw myself rising slowly from bed in a Victorian room that looked medical. I saw myself playing at the playground with my granddaughter. I saw my daughter graduating from college, becoming a teacher. I saw my son working on his first car with me. I saw my wife when I came home. I saw my son graduating from school. I saw our second daughter graduating from school. I saw us happy. I saw myself panicked in the room. I saw the people surrounding me and I saw myself trying to tell them my name. I tried to scream my name but nothing came. I'd been sober for much of my life. I stopped a while before our kids and it only got worse when they left home. First I took a good deal of cough medicine along with my prescriptions. I saw my doctor frequently but wasn't honest when I did. I told her about my anxiety. More Seroquel, more sleep. I took more cough medicine on top of this, over-the-counter stuff. I took Benadryl and I drank quite a bit. My office has a couch in it and lately I'd taken to sleeping there. I stood there drinking from the bottle of vodka and I turned on the television. I saw a father looking at his sleeping family in what must have been Mexico. A show about the border, maybe. I drank and I walked over to the couch and grabbed a tin of tobacco pouches and slid one into my bottom lip and gum. I watched the television and pulled out my phone and idly scrolled through photographs of my family in simpler times as the vodka started to sort of warm my brain. I'd seen this night a million times. I'd played through nights like this a million times. I wanted to throw my typewriter through the window and have it go flying in a darkly lit arc of nightsky before hitting the man-made river floors below. I wanted to spin around with the machine with my fingers jammed between its workings and twirl until prepared to let it fly as a piece of stupid twentieth century shotput. I listened to Smetana. I liked Smetana. I saw Father then and his funeral. I imagined my funeral and I wanted it to be joyous. I wanted the century to end and my children to be happy. I wanted the years to stop moving and I wanted the sky in Idaho to stop being on fire. I wanted my brother near. I wanted my sister near. I wanted to be old and infirm and OK, not a nuisance. I wanted to jump out of the window after the typewriter. I'd read of the French philosopher jumping out the window after his disease overwhelmed him. The pads of his fingers were such that he had to grow his fingernails long so as to be able to type and that sort of thing. I'd always bitten my fingernails. I might've been an old man. I might've been a relapsing drunk. I don't pay attention to these things anymore. I might've not yet been a grandfather. I might've been in St. Elisabeth's, or in the ground, with acorns scattered over me. I still meditated over my death, and it warmed me like the vodka. I thought of running into the window and leaping out into the cold dark night and falling quickly toward the ground. I'm overweight. I eat too much. I've always eaten too much. I'm sixty, I think, I might've been seventy. I can't keep these things straight. I like to stare out the window and imagine I can see what they're making on Mars in the sky. I like to wrap my arms around my wife and give her a long hug. I don't know when this would've been. I don't know that I've kept things exactly in order.

71.

When I think of the events that led to my circumstance as a father, or my circumstance as a husband, I'm often at a loss. I work in design, now, which means I typically balance a small pile of objectives between visualizing someone's ideas or properly writing them out, and it isn't interesting, and I don't love it. I was left with a small bit of money from Father and my wife has a sizable enough savings that we're able to pay for this condominium near downtown in the city. I work to keep insurance. I've always had a number of illnesses related to my skin that make living without insurance an unrealistic proposition, and the diabetes. I'm flailing there maybe. Our children, too, made working a sensible choice as I proved early on to be too frustrated to parent effectively at all hours. I like my life now that I'm free to fall asleep on the couch a bit dosed and enlivened having written a bit and masturbated. I don't know now which is the real me. I stare at the self I've stitched together from fragments and a history and my time when young on the run from life and eventually settling down and developing this family I loved and this marriage to this woman I loved and I don't know if we ever were a part of what happened there. The career was an arbitrary thing. I'd had these little failures and they left me capable of doing academic work and that was about it and after a decade or more of that I think a version of me left or I left and we moved to a place with more vibrance. Suicide, though, has always been with me. I've kept it there like a little fixation I work at day-to-day and sometimes it'll be nourished in my reading, considering the deaths of others and the lives of others and the methods by which they've chosen to reach their ends. I cannot keep the story straight, though, and that's what frustrates me. I don't know where I am in it and I don't know what age I am but I know I'm old and I know I'm taken with various sicknesses and I know I've been married once and I have three children. I've quit my life. I can't keep the whole of it in my mind for any length of time. Father's funeral was... It was... I don't like to think about that time. I don't like to be young again. I don't want to be thirty years old in bed writing this out. I want to be that older me knowing he's near an end. I want the grandchildren to be safe and happy. I don't know where Melody is. I don't know where Flamingo is. I'm a nuisance and a burden. I'm trying to keep my thoughts in order. I'd like to throw the object through the window. I'd like to be the object plummeting toward my death on the concrete. I remember the first time I saw a body that had fallen from a large building and smashed into the pavement and been rearranged there. I walked around taking photos of it when they committed an act of terrorism out West. I think it was out West. I don't think I was in New York for 9/11. The date, 9/11, though, it matters to me, I can't remember why. Greece, I can't remember why. I believe I'm living now and I am near to seventy years old. I believe I'm aging and I believe I'm near to the end of my days.

72.

Some people have very exaggerated ideas about the importance of art. Artists, I think. They need to conceive of art, or writing, as this incredibly important thing, this life-giving life-affirming thing, because anything short of that would mean they were mere dabblers, navel-gazers compared to their friends and family with degrees and jobs as doctors or plumbers, useful things. I used to want to write because for a time I thought of things this way, and then my wife and I had our children, and I looked at the world as someone who was very tired, with not much time in the day to truly spend on myself or whatever I felt interested in, and because of this I realized that the charade put on by most artists, pretending as if their work is impossibly vital to the sustenance of mankind, even while being full of shit, or being sadists, or being violent idiotic people in their daily lives, I realized this charade was all that separated them from the whole of the world, from the very people they purported to understand, and I abandoned that in favor of something else, though I don't recall just what. I don't recall the me of this. I can't. I tried to pay close attention to this and it was difficult. I read about the writer who had left everything behind and become a farmer. I wanted to try and do this, something like this. I took the degrees I had and I tried to get a well-paying job in the city out West and after a while I found one and then I was designing and evaluating technical documents and then my children had grown up and then I was getting older and then we had some horrific fights my wife and I and I believe we separated I cannot be sure though I'm trying to keep everything organized now and it's slipping and I want to hold just one little shard of my history but it keeps eluding me.

73.

If I woke up the next day I got the sense that the entire place was empty. I didn't want to check. I took a quick swig of the vodka and put a plug of tobacco in my lip and I tiptoed through the place to the cupboard where I found some Benadryl. I took eleven of the pink and white capsules with a cup of cold leftover coffee and I walked to the bathroom. It's thanks to my wife that we have this sort of thing, but the bathroom in our condo is one of my favorite places on earth. It's immense, and halved for use on either side by my wife or myself and I like to open myself to it when she's gone and I've got some time. I drank at the cold coffee and turned on the shower in the center of the room. I prepared my razor and some shower gel and I turned on the television set to the right of the entrance to the shower and found some golf, something entrancing, as steam started to lightly coat the place. The Benadryl had begun to work its way into me and I felt simultaneously shot through with speed and ready to sleep for weeks. I dragged the razor over my skin in the heat and when I cut myself slightly on the neck I leaned way back and let the blood flow from me a bit and watched as it mixed with the soap on the floor and spread out. I closed my eyes and sat down on the floor of the shower and turned up the heat as high as it would go and though the water on my back and skull began to burn I didn't stop it. I lay there on the floor and looked up to watch the sky on the golf course as I started to meditate slowly, humming. I was ruminating over my death, and hoping it would come sooner than later. I wasted my life. I have wasted my life. I am in a hammock in Pine Island, Minnesota, or Duluth, Minnesota, or Eau Claire, Wisconsin, or Minneapolis, Minnesota, in the trees, hidden away from things. In Moscow, Idaho. I'm so dumb. Mother, I am dumb. Mutter, I am done. A butterfly is nearby, floating just outside the window and I realize I'm still dead drunk. I can see a large tree out the window that was put there before we moved in. I can feel the life I could've lived. I can feel the life I did live. I can feel the apparatuses of control around me, in my pathetic little hovel. I don't know when I'll see my kids again. I don't know where my granddaughter is. I don't know whether I'm an addict or an alcoholic and I don't know how to have that conversation with my wife, or whether I've already had it, or whether I'm even living as I try and process everything that's going on within my life. *A chicken hawk floats over, looking for home.* I saw an image of the poet James Wright that might not have been James Wright and he was large and looked like most of the men at the meetings I went to in Plymouth, Minnesota when I was young, or Wayzata, Minnesota when I was young, or Center City, Minnesota when I was old again. I am unpacking the ugly minutes of my life and I don't know which way is up. I could've lived forever in Idaho. I could've remained at the university. I could've kept working on something, but I'm not sure what. I don't know what it would've looked like and I don't know how I would've put it out into the world. I'm at a loss. I've wasted my life. Perhaps I wasn't a bad father or a miserable father or a frustrated father or perhaps I was and I didn't see it as a reason to leave the home entirely. I could've stayed home. I might've stayed home. I can't remember anymore. I like to stay home. I can't even remember what day it is now, or what year. I've tried and tried to put it down once and for all but I can't tell. I'm old, and sick, and getting sicker by the day, and I've handed the controls of my life over to others as I can no longer keep things straight. I have wasted my life.

74.

I had friends who coped with their lives and parenting and marriages with more conventional drugs but I've always distrusted access to more conventional drugs. I believe in the person at the door in those situations, sure. I don't believe in what they've got though. I prefer to go to the gas station and narcotize myself. That day I took the Benadryl and dozed off on the floor of the hot shower until my wife found me later with a smear of excrement caked to my ass and stuck because the water couldn't reach it. She told me we were to have dinner with the neighbors, and to clean myself off. I turned the water as hot as it would go and it was still frigid. I showered and watched my filth go down. This sort of putrescence brought me an odd wave of pride. I believe the smell of a person should often be pushed to its limits. I'm not obsessive about showering or anything. I don't want my wife taking care of me this way, in my filth. The thought of it is enough to send me out the window, and it's something I do find myself considering whenever my consciousness is such that I can't really remember when I am. Defenestration, I mean, as an end, defenestration.

75.

Where I'd visited for treatment several times—this place where they'd tried to heal in the manner of the places they'd read about in France, Guattari's places—I can't be sure what happened to the owner there anymore. In 1994 the building was left by a large grocer with ample money who'd decided to remain on the Minnesota side of the river. It sat empty for over a year. It had one floor with sections of basement throughout where storage and freezing would've been, and it was fairly massive. I think he explained this all to me my second day, I could've been forty or forty-five. The grocer tended to find spots where locals from surrounding cities and small midwestern towns could justify drifting in on a weekly or semiweekly basis to purchase large amounts of food and necessities. They'd also secured long-term contracts with several farmers in the same small midwestern cities and towns to supply larger amounts of feed and bedding for animals and the like, which in turn led to their searching the region for ideal locations. Hudson, in Wisconsin, had seemed ideal for its easy access to local communities in Baldwin, say, or Amery, and on the other side in Minnesota there were just as many opportunities. It proved, though, more beneficial to secure a location between Highway 94 and the airport on the Minnesota side, and so the building was left until another large grocer might occupy it or the remnants could be sold off along with the land for some other purpose. This didn't happen at first. Opportunities presented themselves but nothing stuck until one day, Emery, who I think is dead, but I'm not sure, with his ideas about offering treatment to the Wisconsin side and in turn to Chicago, Michigan, Ohio, et cetera, and a massive influx of financing from celebrities who'd worked with him and had their lives changed, as well as funding from the foundation he'd started in 1987 to finance mobile clinics to work with addicts in smaller communities and offer phonelines to those in need, and the location and shape of the structure itself made sense and so the change came. I don't know how many times I've been there. I've visited as an inpatient I think six. I started going when our oldest went away to college and I had a bit of a breakdown. My wife was able to stay with me so we moved back to the Midwest. I think I've been back seven times since, and then I'd visit as well in a more informal sense to talk with Emery, who I also met with via the phone and computer to discuss my issues. I was unhappy at work, terribly unhappy, and I attempted suicide three times throughout my thirties and forties and thus I would return again. Emery formerly went by Simon, I believe, but again I wouldn't swear to it, and I don't have any documentation indicating as much.

76.

In Minnesota treatment centers were like acne. Those in recovery referred to it jokingly as the *land of ten thousand treatment centers*, forgoing its lakes, and this really wasn't far off. Perhaps it was the strange midwestern Protestantism and long winters that made Minnesota such a hub of alcoholism and addiction and their treatment. Nobody's sure, but there they are. Emery didn't have what I'd call confidence in his endeavor. People who no longer took the stuff that they once took to solve the majority—more often all, and creating new—of their problems exuded something that to the straight world looked like confidence, which usually was more like being stripped bare and having no other option but to continue. In the 90s recovery from addiction and alcoholism was dominated as a narrative by someone like a film star or musician from the 70s who had so washed out the whole of their life with cocaine that the only option was a public about-face and a lifetime of tea drinking that really just turned them into someone else. There's also the problem of their money. Emery didn't really have money because what he did have he immediately paid to exes and back into the series of treatment programs and initiatives he was trying to get off the ground, not to make more money but to help people. Alcoholics Anonymous had a strained relationship with Emery because he

wasn't exactly a twelve-step person, but he purchased their literature and encouraged some engagement with it in the early days of
someone's sobriety and so they didn't entirely write him off either.

77.

So this Emery who I think is dead came to Hudson, Wisconsin with a mild comfort in his gut and the sense that he could do something significant here and a view of the long difficulty he had in front of him. I was concerned mainly with the physical space of it. Emery had even hired me for a time to work for him writing their literature and technical documents for the approaches of their nurses, techs, and counselors. It was after one of the stretches I think in my forties and my family had come to live in the Midwest and I had attempted suicide in a hotel room in southern Idaho. The place wasn't run like a hospital or a treatment center. It was run more like a squat. People came to love living there and often would turn right around when kicked out the door to come work as a janitor or tech or in the cafeteria. He received funding because several notable artists and filmmakers had attended in the late 90s and he received a couple of humanitarian awards from local organizations in the Midwest since his patients—a word he wouldn't use—frequently did so much to give back to the surrounding communities. The rate of relapse for anyone who stayed their first twenty-eight days was near to nil, and the only issue became their desire to remain in this place and continue growing and changing accordingly. That's why I returned so much, and it became an issue in my daily life. I think since I had stopped writing really, and sort of left that behind, finding Emery and returning to him and his work was a sort of replacement. I never wrote there, just painted, but the feeling was much the same. Lots of coffee and cigarettes and talking and walking and watching the news and talking some more and going to meetings and going out to bowl or play pool and going out to movies and seeing our families and spending the weekends at some Wisconsin lake with Emery and his third wife and their children. It's hard to shake the notion that this was something I'd imagined. It's hard without the days mapped out there in front of me. There were times in my life where I'd been hospitalized and I know that the majority of them were in the Midwest and I know I knew this Simon and I know I knew this Emery. I don't know how I know the stuff that I seem to know and it doesn't seem to really matter all that much.

78.

Then too the past is always looming there and fragmented scenes are there and if I pull at them they seem to wither off into dust. I like to think back, though, to try and engage these thoughts. I think I'd discussed suicide with Emery, or possibly my wife. I think we talked over this when I was admitted a second time, or when I returned home. I can't be sure. Marriage had grown in and out of favor over the past several decades, and both my wife and I wondered constantly about the choices we'd made when all we wanted to do was scream at one another. Or maybe it isn't there, the past, looming. Maybe the fragmentation is imposed for dramatic effect. Maybe Emery never was and Simon never was and Grant Maierhofer never was. Maybe I'd never discussed suicide or even considered suicide. Maybe I never dumped the orange pills down the toilet in Chicago. Maybe I never turned down anything. Maybe I did everything offered to me and maybe I never winced from living. I don't know. I don't know and I don't know. I don't know why someone's greatest work was left in obscurity in some trunk, only to be published halved years after their death. I wasn't at the Bastille. I never knew Peter Brotzmann. I never knew Gunter Brus. I live in a house somewhere. I go for walks. I eat too much. I go on Weight Watchers. I lie sometimes. I drive poorly sometimes. I've done lots of things I regret. I think I'm seventy years old now. I'm old now. I'm an old man now in my wheelchair at the outskirts of the city square, where he is. I'm seated here now. My wife is with me. My children are with me. I don't know where the manuscript went. I don't have it anymore. I've left it somewhere. I think it burned with some building that burned down. I don't know.

79.

I'm fixated on whether Emery took his own life. While I'm being diagnosed I think, or while our son is being diagnosed. I believe I was being a coward. I believe I might've been hiding in a bathroom. Those weeks in the hospital. The rest of my life stuck within these hospitals. Losing everything. Being ruined. Ruining myself. I can't keep the mess of it clear anymore. I detest my work. I detest the work I've done. I detest the progress I made there with Emery. I detest the fights. I detest the neglect. I detest the times I left my wife to worry over my corpse. I detest the confusion, this ailment, this thing in my rotten putrid skull. I detest being made to stare back at all the treatment centers, and all the hospital wards, and all the doting nurses and the neglectful parents and all the withering misery of it. I detest the scraps of my life there, the meaning. I detest every breathing inch of it, and yet I'm helpless but to watch it undo. The second life seems to become clear, it's yanked by some violent ugly hand. You're stuck. You're watching it play out. Emery killed himself.

80.

The manuscript was never really finished, and seldom really started. What I did first was I sat down in front of the television. I had children, a factor, but they were just as keen as I to sit and watch the images move and speak, so all was well for a time. I'd have to turn it off to change their diapers, and when my wife came home I did my best to perform the identity of a person within this circumstance, but nothing of this nature can really hold, not for long, and so she made me aware, and I apologized. I took to the apologizing, really, and even took to the shouting and the like as it sort of awakened my eyes to the lights of real life, but this, too, had its limits, and so I was forced to change my ways. I wrote an organization because at one point in my history I had studied writing and thought I knew enough to write something significant and was able to convince this organization I was worthy of representation and they were able to sell my ideas for a book to another organization with an advance of six thousand dollars and so I started to work on something that became the manuscript, or maybe this was just writing. It would be the story of my life, a long story, as long as life, and it would conclude on the day on which I'd secured representation for the story itself. I can't discern between families, or histories, or days. Everything sort of boils together in the soup of me and so this might've been when I was twenty-two, this might've been last year, when I was sixty—I believe—this might've been any other time and I was just aware enough to note the shapes of certain things around me. Emery was there, or perhaps Mother was there, or perhaps my wife was there. These are the remaining shadows in my memory. The typewriter, then, and the room, and the vodka, and our granddaughter, but what else. Perhaps the bald counselor was there. Perhaps I was writing there. Perhaps I was awake there to all the possibilities. I can't remember if I quit. I can't remember if I stayed clean. I can't remember if I talked all that much. I remember missing my wife. I remember missing our kids. I remember missing our grandchildren. I remember missing Father. I remember these lights, those lamps, whatever they were. I remember the self there in the center of a room listening to someone talk. I remember my own voice on a recording I heard, telling me something important, some key to all of this. I believe the year was 2019, or later, in 2035, or later still, when the Robert Shields diaries were made available, and I was working at the university there, and I was the first person to read them, I think it was closer to 2050, and I was getting old, and starting to forget, as I am now.

81.

I think maybe I adjusted fairly easily to thinking about death because so much of what I'd seen in life seemed so pathetic and futile. A healthy father suddenly taken by a flaw in his heart while vacationing in Greece. A close friend from youth commits suicide in a horrific manner in response to horrific things in life. Me aging, looking out the window there, not being what I once was and having given up on something I could've lived, a life I could've had. The manuscript, or writing, assembled somewhere, and dumb, and on the floor. It's pathetic, to stare at it there. Emery had a profound ability to tap into what you wished you'd done, to unpack your life in that way, to unpack desire. Now there's only filth. My own life. My filth. My own pathetic selfish yearning. Every step. Every moment. All of it amassed there in front of me. I'm forced to endure it. Masturbating in a dirty bathroom. Calling someone on the phone to tell them you're going to kill yourself. Walking around a city feeling like a spent raw nerve and having no interest in ever being around another human being. Then you have kids and it gets confusing. Your daughter makes you happy. Your son makes you happy. Your second daughter makes you happy. Your son has a debilitating disease you don't understand. You're married. Are you married? Are you a father? Have you done these things? Which you are we talking about?

Which life is this referring to? Why aren't you sure? The end of your life is right there, in the work. It's waiting for you right there to endure and commiserate about it. Maybe when you're down in hell. Maybe when you're kneeling before Lucifer. The name is etched on your gut. Your children won't understand. You'll try and tell them about Kenneth Anger. You tried to tell them about Kenneth Anger. There's Yukio Mishima at his end there. There's all the versions of you amassed there. You're on the beach with Flamingo. You're a father in Idaho. You're living in Hudson and separated from it all. This mortality. This mortal coil. This ridiculous persisting. Trying to figure something out. Taking your medicine. Not getting caught up. Not dwelling on the past. Not panicking about the future. Things are normal. You're medicated. You take antipsychotics and antidepressants and another antidepressant to enhance the abilities of the previous medicines when addressing your obsessive-compulsive disorder. You have obsessive-compulsive disorder. It makes you fearful and doubtful. You drive out of a driveway with a substantial dip and you look back to verify you haven't inadvertently murdered a small child. You look at these possible lives wherein you're plucked from everything. How many marriages? How many lives? How many children? Which you is this? Which one of you is this putting this stuff into the earth? You urinate and become convinced you've urinated someplace inappropriately and are going to be fired for it. You get frustrated and become convinced you're some nightmare of a person. Death, in all of this thinking, would be a welcome relief. Leave home one evening and rent a motel room. Get some drugs and liquor. Relapse. Masturbate to all the things you haven't masturbated to. Eat the Seroquel. Take all the drugs you have and nod off in the bath looking at pictures of your life, or the manuscript. Die.

Acknowledgments

I would like to thank my wife Kelsey and my children first and foremost for always being supportive and helpful. I'd like to thank Jeffrey DeShell, Joanna Ruocco, Dan Waterman and everyone at FC2 and the University of Alabama Press who makes these books possible. I'm also grateful to New Sinews and selffuck, where excerpts from *Shame* previously appeared.